'Now tell me you didn't enjoy that.'

His voice was triumphant, rough with desire.

She trembled, couldn't answer, feeling the aching need inside her.

Stephen's grey eyes probed her face, the parted, trembling curve of her pink mouth, still swollen from his kisses, the wide, darkened blue eyes.

Slowly he said, 'So it isn't being touched that scares you. You aren't scared now, are you? What is it, Gabriella?'

Dear Reader

The Seven Deadly Sins are those sins which most of us are in danger of committing every day: very ordinary failings, very human weaknesses, but which can sometimes cause pain to both ourselves and others. Over the ages they have been defined as: Anger, Covetousness, Envy, Greed, Lust, Pride and Sloth.

In this book I deal with the sin of **Anger**. It is a normal human reaction to get angry when people hurt or offend us, and it helps you get over it if you tell someone they've upset you. It clears the air to tell people how you feel; it makes us understand each other better.

But what happens when anger is hidden or repressed because we are taught to feel guilty about expressing our rage? Or told that it was all our own fault and we deserved what happened? People can spend years with a secret burning rage inside them, torn between guilt and resentment. Sooner or later that rage will either twist a personality and wreck a life, or it will break out in violence.

Charlotte Lamb

This is the sixth story in Charlotte Lamb's gripping seven-part series, *SINS*. Watch out the month after next for the final romance in the set—a complete story in itself—where this exceptionally talented writer proves that love can conquer the deadliest of sins!

Coming in two months' time: HOT BLOOD...the sin of Sloth. Never put off telling someone you love them until tomorrow, when you can tell them today...

Also by Charlotte Lamb:

SECRET OBSESSION...the *Sin* of Pride...
DEADLY RIVALS...the *Sin* of Covetousness...
HAUNTED DREAMS...the *Sin* of Envy...
WILD HUNGER...the *Sin* of Gluttony...
DARK FEVER...the *Sin* of Lust...

ANGRY DESIRE

BY
CHARLOTTE LAMB

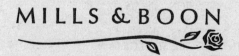

MILLS & BOON

© Charlotte Lamb 1995

ISBN 0 263 79374 5

*Set in Times Roman 10 on 11 pt.
01-9602-50600 C1*

Made and printed in Great Britain

CHAPTER ONE

SHE began to run on the morning of her wedding-day—a cool May morning—before the sun was up.

She had been awake all night, moving restlessly around her Islington flat from room to room, unable to sleep. Each time she caught sight of herself in a mirror she saw the panic in her eyes, their blue so dark that it was almost black. She looked strange, unfamiliar, her face white against the fall of her long, straight black hair, her lips bloodless, quivering.

In a corner of her bedroom on a padded hanger hung the long white dress inside a transparent plastic bag.

'It looks like a butterfly in a cocoon,' Lara had said when she'd come round to see Gabriella two days ago. Her cousin had given her a thoughtful glance. 'Is that how you feel, Gabi? As if you're waiting to break out into a new life? I remember I did. I suppose it's the biggest change in a woman's life, getting married. Life is never the same again.' Then she'd looked more sharply at Gabriella and frowned. 'Are you OK? You don't look like a joyful bride somehow—getting cold feet? We all do, you know.'

'I don't believe you did!' Gabriella had been startled; she would never have expected Lara to have any nerves about anything; her cousin was a capable, confident, assertive woman, just as her mother had been. Nobody ever believed that she and Lara were first cousins. They couldn't have been less alike.

Lara had nodded, looking amused. 'Don't sound so surprised. I'm human too, you know! I remember I was so nervous that I couldn't eat for days beforehand. When I came out of it I was on my honeymoon and starving. I couldn't stop eating; Bob began to think he'd married a food-junkie.'

Gabriella had laughed, but she didn't laugh now as she stared at her wedding-dress. She had bought it in a bridal shop in London; it had caught her eye at once because it was so romantic—white satin and lace, Victorian-style, low at the neck, with a tight waist and a full crinoline-like skirt which had palest pink satin rosebuds scattered here and there.

It had needed some alterations—a tuck here and there—and she had had two fittings before it fitted perfectly, yet now she couldn't remember what she looked like in the dress. She couldn't think of anything but the fear which had begun to tear at her last night, like a wild animal shut inside her breast.

He had noticed, of course; he noticed everything, his narrowed grey eyes searching her face remorselessly, and she hadn't been able to hide her fear or her sick recoil. But all he had said was, 'Get a good night's sleep, Gabriella. Tomorrow is going to be a long day. Just one more day, though, and then we'll have several weeks of sunshine and peace, just the two of us alone.'

He had bent to kiss her again and she had stiffened involuntarily, hearing the echo of his words like a deadly threat. 'Just the two of us alone . . . alone . . . alone . . .'

At least his kiss that time had been as light as the touch of a moth's wing and soon over. She hadn't met his eyes, or looked at the hard, insistent angles of his face.

Gabriella was only five feet two but he was a big man, well over six feet, and although he dressed expensively, in smooth city suits most of the time, the body beneath was lean and spare, powerfully muscled. He had tremendous energy too. She had always known that he was a dynamic man in business—his whole career bore witness to that— but with her he had been different. She had been deceived by his coldly controlled face, and the tight rein on which he kept himself when he was with her. She had got the impression that he was not sexually demanding, that he was not an emotional or passionate man.

How could she have been so blind?

She turned hurriedly, almost falling over one of the expensive leather cases standing near the door, packed ready for departure. Gabriella stared down at them. Her cases had been packed since yesterday, to be collected on the day itself and put into the car which would take them to the airport.

Everything had been carefully planned far ahead, organised down to the last detail by Stephen's secretary, a capable middle-aged woman who had worked for him for years.

Gabriella's passport was in her handbag. Stephen had told her that she needn't bother to bring any money with her, but that had ruffled her sense of independence. She and Stephen were still arguing about her job—he wanted her to stop work when they were married, but she wanted to retain the freedom of being responsible for herself, having her own life outside her home and marriage.

So she had refused to let him give her money before they were married; it would have made her feel as if she was being bought. In her handbag she had a folder full of American dollars which she had got from her own bank; it hadn't left her much in her deposit account, but at least it was hers, so she could take it with her now.

She only had to pick up her cases and walk out, she thought. She didn't have to go through with it. She could just vanish.

Where, though? She had to go somewhere. Her mind worked feverishly. She could take a plane to... No, if she went by air she would have to hire a car and it would be too easy for him to check her name on passenger lists at the airport, and check with car-hire firms.

But would he look for her?

She shivered. He would be so angry. She had seen him lose his temper once when his secretary had had to confess to having mislaid a vital fax. She didn't want that black rage turned on her, and this was much worse than some office mistake. Stephen was going to lose face in a very public way. He would be humiliated, made to look a fool.

He would probably never want to set eyes on her, or even hear her name again.

She choked back a half-hysterical laugh which was also half a sob. No, not him. That much she did know about him. He would want to find her and ... He'll kill me! she thought, her stomach churning.

Think, think! she told herself, trying to clear her weary brain. She had her car. She could just drive out of London and head somewhere quiet and far away ... Cumbria, maybe? Or the far west of Cornwall? Or the Fens? Britain was full of secret, remote places, without railway stations, or hotels, or shopping centres—little villages lost in the countryside, where nothing much ever happened or changed, where few people ever visited.

Oh, but wherever she went in Britain people would read newspapers. She wasn't famous, but Stephen was wealthy and well-known. Some reporter might pick the story up and sell it. Then there would be pictures of her appearing, she would be recognised, and someone unscrupulous who wanted to earn some easy money might ring the Press and tell them where she was, and they would tell Stephen.

No, she must go abroad, as far away as possible. Foreign newspapers wouldn't bother with the story. France was closest; she could easily lose herself in a country as large and as underpopulated as France, but she only knew a little French, and her accent was so atrocious that whenever she tried to say anything in shops or markets crowds of locals gathered to hear her and laugh their heads off at the way she mangled their language.

She didn't have enough money, either, to support herself for very long. She would have to get some sort of work wherever she went, and for that she would have to be able to speak the language. She could get a job in a hotel, maybe, or a restaurant. She was a good cook—she had been well-trained— and they wouldn't insist on references if she offered to show what she could do. But she wouldn't get a job if she couldn't speak the language.

It had to be Italy, then, in spite of the fact that that was where Stephen would expect her to go. Italy, too, was a large country—surely she could hide herself in it somewhere? She would drive down to Dover and buy a ticket for the Channel ferry using cash, making it harder to trace her than if she booked a ticket in advance—she wouldn't show up on the computers until after she had left. Once in France she would make her way on the autoroute into Italy by the most direct route. If she left now she could be in France before Stephen even knew she had gone.

Her mother had been Italian, and Gabriella had been born there and lived there until she was eleven and her mother had died. She had dual nationality and spoke the language fluently. She would not stand out in Italy; she could easily be taken for a native.

She wouldn't be able to go anywhere near Brindisi, where her mother had come from—there were only distant relatives living there now, but Stephen knew about them, and would look there first. She would make for the northern part of Italy, as far away from Brindisi as possible.

She hurried into her bathroom and, dragging her nightdress over her head, stepped into the shower. The sting of the water sharpened her mind; a few minutes later she towelled herself dry and began to dress.

First she put on black lace panties and a matching bra, and then old blue jeans and a thin blue cotton sweater. She didn't want to be noticed; she would pass without comment in her old clothes, and they would be comfortable for travelling.

Her long black hair she put up in a knot at the back of her neck, but she put on no make-up, not even a touch of lipstick. She would wear dark glasses as she drove and keep them on as she crossed the Channel—that would help keep her anonymous.

She mustn't be recognised anywhere on the way because Stephen was going to be right behind her, and the very thought of him scared her stiff.

Oh, God, why didn't I face it long ago? she inwardly wailed, shivering.

What would he do to her if he caught up with her? Last night she had seen the real Stephen, the nature he had hidden from her all these months. She wasn't blinkered any more—she knew she could expect no mercy from him.

She had to let him know in advance, even so; she couldn't just run away and leave him standing at the altar not knowing what had happened to her. She sat down at a table and scribbled a note to him. There was no time to pick and choose her words, to break it tactfully; she simply told him that she was very sorry, please to forgive her, but she couldn't go through with it, and was going away.

She began to fold the note, then on an afterthought added a few more lines.

Please let everyone know and make my apologies. Try to understand, Stephen—I'm sorry, I just can't marry you after all. I thought I could, but I can't. I'm sorry, I can't explain.

She signed it with her name in a scrawl then read it and groaned. It was incoherent—he would think she'd been drunk when she wrote it, but it was the best she could do, and there was no time to try again.

She would put it into his mail-box at the apartment block on her way out of town—she knew the porter delivered all mail at eight o'clock, which was around the time the post office delivered it.

The wedding was due to take place at eleven-thirty—Stephen would have time to cancel the service and the reception before people began arriving. At least he would have help—he had a huge secretarial team in his offices; they could make the phone calls for him. Even so, she flinched from the thought of the chaos that was going to follow: the presents that would have to go back, the three-tiered bridal cake that nobody would want now, all the food for the reception.

It was going to be embarrassing and humiliating for Stephen and she felt a weary sense of shame at doing this to him as she stared down at the envelope on which she had written his name and address.

For a second she couldn't decide what to do, then the panic began to burn in her stomach again and she swung away. She could not go through with it, that was all. Whatever the consequences, she could not marry him.

To calm herself, she concentrated on little details—went through her handbag to check that she had everything she would need, then put on a light summer jacket—black and white striped. Picking up her car keys, she was about to let herself out of the flat when she saw some letters on a table; she had written them yesterday morning, and forgotten to post them. Automatically she picked them up and was about to put them into her bag when her eye fell on the address on the top letter.

At that second, inspiration hit her. Paolo! In his letter he had said that he was staying at a villa on Lake Como; he would be there all summer, until September; he was painting a series of frescos on the walls of a small private theatre in the villa, which was owned by a world-famous opera director who liked to try out future productions in his own theatre.

It was like a signpost blazing her path. That's it, I'll go to the Italian Lakes, she thought. They're hundreds of miles north of Brindisi. Stephen isn't likely to think of looking there—why should he? I've never told him how important Paolo is to me.

Dropping the envelopes into her handbag, she let herself out of the little flat on the ground floor of an old Victorian house. Her car was parked in what had once been the front garden; now, covered in asphalt, it served as a car park for the tenants of the flats into which the house had been divided.

It was five-thirty in the morning; London was grey and dim, with few cars around, and even fewer people. The street-lights glowed yellow as she headed south towards the river. She pulled up beside a red postbox which she saw on a corner, and posted all the letters except the one to Paolo. There was so little traffic that it only took her ten minutes after that to reach the apartment block facing Hyde Park with views of the cool green shade under the trees.

It had been one of Stephen's most prestigious projects, built five years ago right in the heart of London's most expensive and fashionable area, with marvellous views. Even a small flat there cost the earth.

Stephen had moved into the penthouse apartment as soon as the building had been completed; he had always meant to live there, he had told her. He had worked on the specifications of the penthouse with the architect with his own tastes in mind, and had chosen the décor, creating a perfect home for himself.

Beyond his long, beautifully furnished lounge lay a broad terrace garden; it even had small trees growing in pots, and shrubs and flowers which breathed fragrance at night. She had loved walking out there at night, watching London far below, the sound of it muted, unreal.

Being so close to the park was wonderful too, almost giving one the feeling of being in the country. On hot days you could get cool in the shade of the trees, have a picnic, or row on the Serpentine. Stephen rode in Hyde Park at weekends, on a big black Arab horse which he kept in stables near by, and in the early mornings he jogged in a tracksuit to keep fit, following the twisting paths under the trees for half an hour.

It was lighter when she parked outside the apartment block, knowing that there were unlikely to be police around at that hour. It was the work of a minute to run across the pavement and drop her letter into the chrome letter-box on the front of the locked bullet-proof glass doors of the block.

The porter seated behind his desk looked up, recognised her, looked startled, but immediately gave a polite smile, and stretched his hand out ready to press the button that would open the doors electronically, if she wished, but she shook her head and turned away.

Behind her she sensed him walking towards the doors to collect the letter she had delivered.

Please don't take it up at once! she thought, her heart going like a steam-hammer.

He wouldn't, though, surely? Not at this hour! He would keep it and take it up with the rest of Stephen's mail.

Although it was cool she was sweating as she got back into her car. She slammed the door, put on her seatbelt, and then risked a glance upwards to the soaring top of the forty-storey block, to where the penthouse rose against the early morning sky.

She had expected the high, wide windows to be dark too, but they blazed with light. Shock hit her. Stephen must be awake. Couldn't he sleep either? It hadn't occurred to her that he might be nervous too; might have doubts or uncertainties.

A shadow moved at one of the windows and her throat closed in fear. Was that him? Or was she imagining it? It was so far up that she couldn't be sure. Was he looking out? Looking down? What if he saw her? What if he had spotted the car? Was he watching her, wondering what she was doing out there, and if she was coming up? Would he come down to find out if she had left a message?

Her hands shaking, she started her engine and stepped on the accelerator, shooting away as if the devil himself were after her.

She drove far too fast in sheer panic but there were no police cars around to notice her. She shot through comparatively empty streets down to the softly moving Thames with its glittering reflections of light from the embankment and the high-rise office blocks on each bank. A few moments later she was across Westminster Bridge, and driving into the southern suburbs, unnaturally quiet at this hour, the normally crowded roads almost empty, just the odd car passing her, and a bus lumbering into the city with a few sleepy passengers, workmen on their way home after a night shift.

I won't ring Paolo from England, I'll make for Lake Como, she thought. I'll book into a hotel, and only then get in touch; that will be safest.

She had written to tell him that she was getting married and to invite him to the wedding but he had written back to say he was sorry but he couldn't make it. He had hoped that she would be happy, and he had sent her an exquisite piece of Venetian glass—a candelabra, frosty and twisting, a centre-piece for a dinner-table, he'd said. She had only received it yesterday and she hadn't yet told Stephen about it.

She didn't remember mentioning Paolo to him at all, but his name had been on the list of wedding invitations under his home address in Rome. Stephen probably wouldn't have noticed it, except to assume that he was one of her Italian relatives, and in a sense that was close in the truth. Paolo meant more to her than any of them ever had, anyway.

She arrived at Dover with half an hour to wait before she could board the ferry, and she had had time to think while she drove. So when she bought her ticket she managed to get some loose change, went to a phone box in the ferry terminal, and rang Lara.

The ringing went on for a long time before a sleepy voice finally came on the line, growling, 'Who...?'

'Lara, it's me, Gabriella,' she began, and Lara gave an outraged squawk.

'You're kidding! Gabi, what the hell do you mean by ringing me at...? Where's that damned clock...? Good grief, it's only seven-thirty! Do you know what time I went to bed? Five minutes ago! Tommy's new tooth decided to come through last night; he cried and yelled until he was tomato-red and I was as limp as lettuce. He only went to sleep as it began to get light, the little monster. So, whatever the crisis, you'll have to cope with it without me. I need some sleep before I even think about getting ready.'

Before she could hang up Gabriella said huskily, 'I'm not getting married today, Lara.'

A silence. 'What?'

Gabriella talked fast to stop her from inter-
rupting. 'I'm going away. I've written to Stephen.
I'm sorry, I can't explain—I have to go, but will
you tell the others? Say I'm sorry, I'm really sorry,
but I just can't go through with it.'

She ran out of words then and hung up, but not
before hearing her cousin burst out, 'Where are you
going? What...?'

Gabriella stared at her face reflected in the
perspex hood over the phone. With her black hair
pulled back off her forehead and no make-up on
her face, she looked even younger, her eyes a
turmoil of feelings that she had kept shut down for
years and was still terrified of confronting.

I must cut my hair! she thought. It is far too
long. I'll have it cut short as soon as I get to France.

She bought a cup of hot black coffee from a stall
and drank it in her car, staring at the waiting lines
of cars ahead of her. They finally began to move
and she followed them up into the ferry, parked as
commanded by the seaman in charge and went up
into the ship.

She couldn't have eaten to save her life. She sat
out on deck and watched the green hills of England
fade into the distance as they sailed. It was a very
short trip—just an hour and a half.

She drove off in Calais and followed the road
system circling the old town—it was amazing how
quickly one got out of Calais and got on to the
motorway to Paris.

By half-past eleven—the hour when she would
have been walking up the aisle towards Stephen—

she was well on her way towards Paris. After checking the map, she had decided that she could not face driving across the mountains, through Switzerland, via the Simplon Pass, which would probably be a hair-raising experience for an inexperienced driver. Instead she headed for the Autoroute du Sud for Menton and the Italian border. It was a long way round, but the terrain would be easier to handle.

She could not make the trip in one day—it was around seven hundred miles. She drove until she was dropping with exhaustion and then looked for a motorway hotel for the night. By then she was well past Lyon.

She ate a light meal in the hotel restaurant— melon followed by a goat's cheese salad—then went to bed. The room was sparsely furnished with a bed, one uncomfortable chair, and a rail for clothes, and there was a tiny shower-room with a lavatory. At least that was clean and very modern. It cost her very little, and she could have slept on the floor, she was so weary.

Even so, she woke up several times with bad dreams, trembling and sweating, remembering only Stephen's face, haunted by it.

The last time she woke it was half-past five so she showered, got dressed and went to have breakfast. It was better than the evening meal. The coffee was strong, there was orange juice and compotes of real fruit, the rolls were freshly cooked, and there were croissants and little pots of jam.

Gabriella drank juice and several cups of coffee, but only one croissant. Then she checked out, paid

her bill by credit card, because it would take some
time for the details to reach England, and then set
off again, into a blue and gold morning, heading
south. The further she went, the warmer the
weather became. The landscape changed all the
time, from the deciduous trees and green fields of
mid-France to the cypress, olives and herb-scented
maquis of Provence.

The motorway curved round from Provence
towards the Côte d'Azur; the sky was a deep
glowing blue, and now and then she saw the sea on
her right, even deeper blue and glittering with sunlight. She drove through the low green foothills of
the Alpes-Maritimes, saw the red roofs and white
walls of villas lining the slopes of the hills and tum-
bling down towards the sea.

It looked so lovely that she was tempted to stay
there a night or two. By then she was tired again,
and in a mood to weep like a child, but she forced
herself to push on and in the late afternoon she
crossed the border into Italy at Menton, and turned
up north again, away from the sea and the Italian
Riviera, towards Milan and the Italian Lakes. She
was turning back on herself, but the road was half-
empty and she made good speed—it was still faster
than trying to use a more direct route.

Driving became more difficult after she left the
motorway and found herself on the narrow,
twisting, traffic-laden roads running around the
glimmering waters of Como, set like a blue mirror
between jagged mountains.

She was almost hallucinating by then, driving like
an automaton, barely aware of her surroundings

and beginning to be afraid that she would crash. She must stop, must find a hotel, she thought stupidly, trying to stay awake.

She didn't know the area at all and had no idea which hotel to check into, but when she found herself driving past a hotel entrance she simply spun the wheel and turned in through the old black wrought-iron gates, followed by the angry horn blasts of other drivers who had been startled by her sudden move.

It was obviously an old grand hotel, now a little shabby but still glittering with chandeliers and marble floors, set in well-kept gardens, looking out across Lake Como which she could see through the trees running down the sides of the hotel.

There were other cars parked echelon-style on the gravelled drive; she pulled in beside one of them. Before getting out her case she walked unsteadily into the hotel reception area feeling almost drunk with tiredness.

The reception clerk behind the polished mahogany counter looked up politely and shot an assessing glance over her jeans and old jacket, his face cooling.

'*Sì, signorina*?' He had apparently even noticed the lack of a wedding-ring on her hand.

Gabriella found herself beginning to answer in easy Italian. She hadn't forgotten her mother's tongue, then! She explained that she was travelling and needed a room for a night or two, that her car was parked outside, with her luggage inside it.

The clerk looked sceptical but offered her a printed brochure which gave the prices of the

rooms, perhaps expecting her to be taken aback by
the high cost of staying there, and Gabriella gave
it a cursory glance, nodding, not really caring how
much it cost. She had to get some sleep and she
wasn't short of cash, thank heavens.

'Do you have a room facing the lake?'

'A single room?'

'Please.'

'How will you be paying, *signorina*?' the clerk
warily enquired.

'Cash, in advance,' Gabriella said, getting out a
wallet and laying down the price of the room for
that night.

The clerk considered the money. 'You do not
have a credit card?'

'Certainly,' she said, showing it to him. He picked
it up and checked the details on it. 'But I wish to
pay cash for tonight. If I decide to stay longer, and
you have a room available, I may use my credit
card for any larger amounts. Is that a problem?'

He looked puzzled but shook his head, gave her
back her credit card and the usual card every guest
had to fill in, asked to see her passport and looked
even more startled as she gave him the Italian one.

'You are Italian?' That told her that her accent
wasn't quite as good as she had thought it was.

Quietly she explained, 'I was born here, but I
live in Britain. My father was British, my mother
Italian, so I have dual nationality.'

He handed her back the passport, a smile finally
crossing his face. 'Then I do not need to keep this.'
He picked up her money and handed her a key. 'I

hope you have a very pleasant stay with us, *signorina*. Would you like help with your luggage?'

'Please,' she said, handing him the key of her car. 'Just the smaller tan leather case, please.'

She went to the room and immediately plunged her sweating face into cool, clear water. What she wanted was a bath, but that could wait until her luggage arrived and she could unpack clean clothes to change into.

The porter brought her case; she tipped him generously, got a broad grin and asked him to book her in for dinner for the evening.

When she was alone again she stripped and had a long, relaxing bath, put on a white cambric dress, the bodice stiff with broderie anglaise, and lay down on the bed, her muscles weak and her ears singing with hypertension.

She couldn't remember ever having been this tired before! She wanted to go to sleep, but first she had to ring Paolo.

It was surely many months since she had last spoken to him. They were neither of them great letter writers, and anyway theirs was a very intermittent friendship; it was often several years before they got in touch, but the minute they did it was as if they had never been apart.

She had always been able to tell Paolo everything. At least she would be able to talk to him about what was tearing her apart, be open about why she could not go through with her marriage, knowing that he would understand. He was the one person in the world whom she had ever told about the past.

Paolo had lived next door to her when she was a child. He was four years older than she and had been a short, dark, silent boy, always painting and drawing and making clay figures. They had been thrown together because their mothers had been friends and neither of them had found it easy to get on with their own classmates.

Gabriella, shy and nervous, had found Paolo's silences reassuring; he was sensitive and intelligent, and very different from the other boys in his class at school. They had mostly been bigger, cheerfully down-to-earth, and had made fun of his passion for art, despised him because he didn't love football and fighting, and bullied him a little too. Paolo had kept away from them whenever he could; he had already had a sure sense of what he wanted and had known that it would take him away from Brindisi.

When Gabriella's mother died, her grieving father had taken his daughter back to England so that he could be near his only living relative, his mother. Jack Drayton was himself a man in poor health; he had only survived his wife by three years and had usually been too ill to see much of his only child.

Gabriella had been sent away to boarding-school, although she'd spent her summers with her father's brother Ben and his family. They had given her a couple of very happy years until it had all crashed down again. Sometimes she'd thought that every time she began to be really happy fate intervened—something always happened to wreck it.

Her uncle Ben had died suddenly the summer that she was fourteen. Afterwards his wife had sold their home, taken her children and gone back to Scotland, to the village where she had been born. After that, Gabriella had stayed with her grandmother, her father's mother, in the summer.

During all those years, Gabriella had written to Paolo and got back scratchy little notes from him, but she hadn't actually seen him again until he had come to England on holiday five years ago. She had still been at school, and was spending the holidays with her grandmother in Maidenhead on the River Thames—and she had been thrilled to see Paolo again.

He had stayed in London for a fortnight. Gabriella had shown him around, taken him to Windsor and Hampton Court, Kew Gardens and as far afield as Stratford-on-Avon, so that he could visit the theatre and see Shakespeare's birthplace and Anne Hathaway's cottage.

Paolo had just left art school in Milan and was going to be taking up a career in TV, set-designing. At twenty-one, he had been far more sophisticated and worldly-wise than the seventeen-year-old Gabriella, yet somehow they had picked up their brother-sister relationship where it had left off six years earlier without any difficulty.

When he'd gone back to Milan he'd rarely written. Neither had, but she'd known that when she saw him again they would still talk the same language—indeed, understand each other without words.

Smiling, she picked up the phone and dialled his number. The ringing went on for quite a while before his voice came on the line.

'*Sì?*' He sounded impatient; perhaps he was very busy.

'Paolo?' she whispered uncertainly, and heard his intake of breath.

'Where are you?'

His swift reply told her a lot. 'You know?'

Paolo didn't bother to ask what she meant. His voice dry, he said, 'He rang me last night. Even over the phone he was quite frightening. I don't know what he does to you, but he turned my blood to ice. I got the distinct impression that if he found out I'd lied to him he would tear my head off my body and then dance on the rest of me.'

She half laughed, half sobbed. 'How did he get your number?'

'I think he was trying everyone you ever mentioned to him. No stone unturned, Gabi.'

She had known what he would do. Wearily she said, 'I barely mentioned you to him.'

'*Mia cara*, I was on your guest list!'

'Yes, you were, but how did he find you so quickly? I gave him your address in Rome.'

'Unfortunately, he—or one of his staff—knew I worked for TV in Rome, and tried them. Of course, they knew where to find me; I'd left my summer address with them.'

She sighed, closing her eyes. 'Thank God I didn't ring you before I left—at least you really weren't lying when you told him you didn't know where I was. Do you think he believed you?'

'I think he must have realised that I was surprised. Yes, I think he believed I didn't know where you were, but I may have spoilt the effect later—I lost my temper, I'm afraid.'

Anxiously she asked, 'What did you say to him?'

'I told him I wouldn't tell him even if I did know where you were, but I hadn't heard a word from you so I didn't have to lie and I said that if you did get in touch I certainly wouldn't tell him so he could shove off.' Paolo sounded triumphant. 'He didn't like that, I'm glad to say. I did not take to him, *mia cara*—in fact, I disliked him intensely from the first word he uttered, and, whatever happened, I'm on your side.

'Come here if you want to; I'll give you sanctuary. You'll be quite safe here—the grounds are patrolled by mad packs of hounds at night and the gates and walls are electrified—he won't get in.'

Her pale mouth curved into a smile. 'You're a darling, Paolo. Listen, your phone might be bugged by now—he's quite capable of it and he can afford to hire detectives who'll do that. I'll write. I'm OK, don't worry. Bye.'

She hung up and lay staring at the ceiling. She would go down and get a postcard of the hotel; she had seen some on the reception desk. She would write a few apparently innocent words on it. 'Having a lovely time, wish you were here!' She would sign it, not with her name but with the word *cara*. It should reach him tomorrow. Paolo was quick-witted; he would understand at once and come to the hotel to find her.

She only hoped that Stephen had believed him and was looking for her somewhere else.

CHAPTER TWO

GABRIELLA woke next morning to the sound of a church bell chiming seven. An echo came from across the lake—or was that another church telling the hour? For a moment she lay there, dazedly remembering the incoherent dreams she had been haunted by all night—Stephen's hard, dark face, his mouth, the heat of his body moving against hers, his hands...

Perspiration broke out on her forehead. With a low groan she sat up in bed and looked around the room. The walls were whitewashed. Last night they had looked rather stark, but this morning they were coloured pinky gold by the sun. She had not closed her shutters last night and had left the window slightly ajar; a gentle breeze was now ruffling the floor-length white gauze curtains.

Gabriella slid out of bed in her thin silky nightdress and walked over to the window, pushed it right open and went out on to her balcony, to be struck dumb by the beauty of the view.

She stood there, staring, blue eyes wide; she hadn't expected anything like this. Her gaze moved over the ring of mountains, their indented line blue-hazed, majestic, stretching away out of sight, the morning light moving on their peaks where here and there snow still covered the upper slopes, a cloudless sky floating above them and below, on the surface of the lake, their shimmering reflections, white, gold and soft rose.

Como was not a huge lake; it had a domestic intimacy, and she could see the other side of it clearly enough to make out houses, red-roofed and white-walled, gardens with cypress and fir trees, and, on the winding roads along the lakeside, cars moving.

The hotel gardens ran right down to the lake to where she saw a wooden jetty, with a few people waiting on it—men reading newspapers, schoolchildren, women with shopping baskets chatting to one another. On the lake a small ferry boat was chugging towards them at a sedate speed. She watched it dock, nudging the old tyres tied along the jetty. A sailor tied up and the passengers boarded, greeting the jerseyed sailors on board like old friends—which they probably were.

The boat cast off again, crossing the lake again. Gabriella watched it leave. She could see why people who lived here would use the ferry if they wanted to cross the lake. Driving around those narrow, twisting little roads would be hair-raising even in daylight. That's what I'll do, she thought; I'll leave my car at the hotel and explore the lake on the ferry.

She heard cheerful, murmuring voices outside in the corridor, then the whirr of the lift descending—other people going to breakfast, obviously—which reminded her that she had ordered a breakfast-tray in her room for eight o'clock. Taking a last look at the view, she turned reluctantly away into her bedroom.

She showered, slid into a towelling robe hanging on the door and sat on the bed to blow-dry her long, silky hair; it took quite a time, so in the end she left it loose, to finish drying naturally, and dressed in a dark blue linen shift dress, leaving her slender legs bare but sliding her feet into white sandals with a tiny heel, a few fine straps of leather criss-crossing the foot, buckled at the ankle.

A few moments later the room-service waiter tapped on her door. He was a young boy in a spotless white uniform, as slender as a girl and doe-eyed. He gave her an appreciative look, young though he was—he was, after all, an Italian and enjoyed the sight of a pretty woman. 'Your breakfast, *signorina*,' he said smiling as she admitted him.

'*Grazie*,' she said, leading the way out on to the balcony. In Italian she told him to put the tray down on the small white table.

'A lovely morning for you,' he said, as if he had produced that too. His dark eyes admiringly flicked over her from her black hair to her long legs. Clearly he was in no hurry to leave. 'Is this your first visit to Como?'

'Yes, and I've never seen anything so beautiful. Where does the ferry go?' she asked, pointing to the jetty where a new string of passengers was boarding a different boat.

'That one?' He gave it an indifferent glance. 'That sails between Menaggio, Bellagio and Varenna.'

'Do all the ferries have the same route?'

'Oh, no—some go right the way to Como itself, at the far end of one arm of the lake...'

'One arm?' she asked, puzzled.

'The lake is a Y-shape, *signorina*.' He pulled a pencil from his pocket and drew a rough outline on a notepad he also carried. 'Like that. Como is at the end of this upper arm and Lecco is almost at the end of the other arm. The lake divides at Bellagio, then you come down here to Novate.'

'What a strange shape for a lake! So which town is this?'

He gave her a startled look, his great dark eyes incredulous. 'This is Menaggio, *signorina*! You didn't know that?'

She grinned at him. 'I drove in here on impulse last night; I was so tired that I didn't even notice the name of the hotel, let alone the place.'

The boy was in no hurry to leave. 'Where do you come from? I don't recognise your accent. You sound southern—are you from Naples?'

She laughed. 'Close—I was brought up in Brindisi.'

Another waiter appeared below, on the terrace steps, and whistled piercingly. The boy looked down, startled, was given a peremptory gesture and an angry glare, and hurriedly turned away.

'I must go... Excuse me, *signorina*.'

He vanished and, smiling wryly to herself, Gabriella sat down and considered her breakfast-tray—a glass of orange juice embedded in a bowl of crushed ice, a silver coffee-pot, rolls, a couple of little cakes, butter, a pot of jam, a bowl of fresh black cherries and some frosted green grapes.

She didn't touch the cakes, but she ate a roll and some of the cherries, drank all the juice and a couple of cups of coffee while she gazed down at the lake, watching the changing reflections until a passing boat sent wide ripples to break them up. People on the jetty were talking to each other cheerfully, their voices drifting to her on the warm air. She thought that it must be nice to live in a small place where you knew everyone; big cities like London could be lonely places.

The telephone made her jump. She turned her head to stare at it in terror.

Who could be ringing her? Nobody knew she was there. Her heart began to beat agonisingly; her skin tightened and turned icy cold. She was trembling as she got up, knocking over the chair she had been sitting on.

The phone still went on ringing; maybe it was the hotel reception desk asking if she was staying another night. Slowly, reluctantly, she crossed the room and stretched out a shaky hand.

'Hello?' Her voice was low, husky.

'Signorina Brooks?' an Italian voice asked.

'Yes.' She was waiting on tenterhooks.

'A Signor Giovio to see you, *signorina*.'

She let out a quivering breath, closing her eyes in sick relief. It was only Paolo; he had got her card already and understood its message. She had known he would—he was much too quick not to have got it at first glance. 'Oh...my cousin, yes; tell him I'll be down in a moment.'

She brought her tray into her bedroom, then closed the balcony doors and almost flew downstairs. Paolo was waiting for her in the lounge which led out on to the garden terrace.

The room was enormous, with high ceilings from which glittered chandeliers and marble floors across which deep white sofas were scattered. One end was entirely made up of windows, stretching from ceiling to floor, draped in the same white gauze curtains as those which hung in her room; through them you could see the hotel gardens leading down to the lake and they allowed the sun to flood the great room with light.

Paolo stood by them, gazing out. She stopped to stare at him while he was unaware of her. He hadn't changed much since they'd last met although he was clearly a few years older. He was still a slight figure, his face in profile bony and memorable—not handsome but striking, his sallow skin deeply tanned and his hair jet-black, softly waving down to his shoulders. He was wearing a lightweight pale blue suit; elegantly casual, it looked expensive. Did he buy designer clothes now?

As if becoming aware of her presence he turned, their eyes met and a smile lit his thin face. 'So, there you are!' he said in Italian, holding out both hands, and she ran to take them.

'I knew you'd understand the card.'

'Of course,' he dismissed, shrugging. His slanting eyes skimmed her face. 'You don't look as terrible as you sounded last night. Sleep well?'

She nodded but perhaps the memory of her bad dreams showed in her face, because Paolo frowned.

Some other guests wandered into the room, giving them curious looks. Gabriella opened the tall glass door into the garden.

'Let's walk by the lake. I'm dying to get a closer look at it. Isn't it breathtaking? How long have you been here?'

'A couple of weeks.' Paolo fell into step beside her as she began to descend the stone steps towards the lakeside. 'Are you going to tell me about it?'

She stopped on the jetty and leaned on the wooden rail, staring out towards another town on the far side of the lake. 'Where's that?' she asked, pointing.

'Varenna,' Paolo said in a dry tone, knowing that she was delaying any more intimate talk.

'Is it worth visiting?'

'It's small but pretty; there are some nice gardens to see. Are we going to talk about the scenery or are you going to tell me why you ran away?'

She went on staring across the lake and didn't answer.

Paolo drew a folded newspaper from under his arm and offered it to her. Frowning, Gabriella took it, looked at the front page and with a leap of the nerves saw that it was an English paper.

'Page five,' he said.

Hands trembling she turned the pages and saw her own face, grey and blurred, in a photo which she didn't remember being taken—she and Stephen arriving at a theatre for a very starry first night. Feverishly she skimmed the story; it was short on facts but those it had were mostly about Stephen and it pretended sympathy for him at being left at the altar.

Somehow the reporter made her sound like a bimbo—a gold-digger who had probably run off with an even richer man, although none was actually suggested. The story did, however, claim that she had not sent back her engagement ring, which was worth hundreds of thousands of pounds, and added that she had got other valuable jewellery out of Stephen, all of which she had also kept.

She crushed the paper in her hands and looked at Paolo, stricken. 'You bought this here?'

He nodded. 'There's a good newsagent who sells a few foreign newspapers. This was the only popular English paper on sale this morning but he said he'd had half a dozen copies of this one. If you look at the date you'll see that it was out in England yesterday.'

Pale, she said, 'So others may have read the story.'

Paolo nodded grimly and took the screwed-up paper, smoothing it out again to study Stephen's face in the grey photo. 'Is it a good likeness?'

She glanced at the hard face, the fleshless cheek-bones, the cool grey eyes, that insistent jawline. A little shiver ran through her.

'Yes.'

Paolo screwed the newspaper up again and tossed it into a nearby refuse bin.

'What did he do to you?'

She gave a choky little sigh. 'Nothing—nothing at all. Poor man, he must be utterly bewildered—that's why I couldn't tell him face to face.'

'That would have been an idea,' Paolo said without inflexion.

She flinched as if from an accusation, guilt in her eyes, and shot him a distraught look. 'I know— I know I should have, but I couldn't, I just couldn't talk to him. He would never have understood unless I told him...and I couldn't talk about it, Paolo; I still can't talk about it.'

'Ah,' he said on an indrawn breath. 'So. That is what it is all about.'

She turned to look at him, her eyes glistening with unshed tears. 'Oh, you're so quick; you always know what I'm talking about. That's why I came here to find you—at least you'll understand. I can talk to you without having to dot every I and cross every T.'

He touched her cheek with one fingertip. 'I had a suspicion that this might be behind it, but it's years ago—you should have had therapy, you know, talked it out with a professional.'

'I couldn't.' Her pink mouth was stubborn, unhappy. The breeze blew her black hair across her cheek and she brushed it away angrily.

'That's just why you ought to try!'

'Anyway, nothing really happened. I'm not the victim of some horrible crime.'

'Crimes of the heart can be as disastrous.'

Another sigh shook her. 'Yes. Don't let's talk about it.'

He grimaced. 'OK. Tell me how you met this guy Stephen Durrant, then—tell me about him. He didn't make a great impression on me on the phone.'

She turned and walked further along the lake, under a line of magnolia trees in bloom, their flowers perched like great white birds on the glossy green leaves.

'Stephen heads a big property company...DLKC Properties. I don't expect you'll have heard of them.'

'I have,' Paolo said, shooting a narrowed glance at her. 'So he's behind them, is he? I thought they were an international consortium.'

'They are, but Stephen is the main shareholder.'

'He must be very rich, then. They weathered the storm when property took a nosedive a few years back. A lot of other companies were wiped out but DLKC survived intact.

'A friend of mine bought a flat in a block they built in Tenerife—it was brilliantly designed, and a nice place to live, I thought. The landscaping was excellent—well laid out gardens, a nice-sized pool...' He stopped and grinned down at her. 'Sorry; you know how obsessed I am with design.'

'I remember,' she said, smiling back. 'And you know I love my work too. I'm always sorry for people who don't enjoy their job.'

'Does Stephen Durrant enjoy his?'

She couldn't put Paolo off the scent. She looked at him wryly.

'Stephen lives for his work; he rarely has time for anything else.'

'Including you?'

She looked away, across the lake. 'He made time for me. When he remembered.'

'Ah,' Paolo said again. 'Did that make you angry?'

'Angry?' She was taken aback by the question. 'Why should it?'

But hadn't she resented the fact that Stephen had so little time and saw her so rarely? At the same time, though, she had been relieved, because she was afraid of him getting too close, becoming too important to her. Afraid of him, of herself.

Why are you such a coward? she thought wildly. Why are you so scared of everything?

'He has a reputation as a bit of a hard man, doesn't he?' murmured Paolo, watching her troubled face.

She turned away, picked a leaf from a bush and crumpled it in her cold hands, inhaling the aromatic scent of the oils released.

'Well, he's very successful. I suppose most successful people are pretty tough.'

Paolo nodded thoughtfully. 'Is he a self-made man? He sounds like one.'

'He built his business up himself, but he inherited a small building firm from an uncle when he was twenty.'

'How old is he now?'

'Thirty-six.'

'Did the age-gap bother you?'

She shook her head. 'I've never been interested in anyone my own age; I prefer older men.' She stopped dead, catching Paolo's eyes, and flushed scarlet, then went dead white. Hurriedly she walked on and he caught up with her.

After a moment or two he said, 'But you're scared of Stephen, aren't you?'

'If you knew him, you'd be scared of him.'

'Then why in God's name did you agree to marry him?'

'I don't know,' she wailed, her face working in anguish.

'Surely to God you knew how you felt about him, Gabriella?' Paolo sounded impatient, angry with her, and that made her feel worse. She was terrified of angry scenes, of someone looking at her accusingly, blaming her. Tears stung her eyes.

'I felt…safe…with him…' she whispered, and Paolo was silent for a moment.

'What changed?'

She didn't answer, looking away.

Paolo said, 'I take it that he is in love with you?'

Her long black hair blew across her face again, in blinding strands, and she didn't push it away this time. Her eyes hidden, she whispered, 'I don't know.'

Paolo's voice hardened. 'Oh, come on, *mia cara*, you must know how he feels about you!'

She knew Stephen wanted her physically—that fact had been blazingly obvious when he had lost control and started making love to her with that terrifying heat. She shivered. He had never been like that before. Why that night?

But she knew why; she had known at the time although in her sheer blind panic she hadn't allowed herself to think about her own guilt. Now she did, and Paolo frowned as he watched her changing, disturbed face.

'Don't look like that. It can't be that bad!'

Can't it? she thought, staring across at the sunlit, white-capped mountains and remembering her mood that last evening. She had been edgy, shy, uneasy, but she had tried to hide it because she and Stephen had been the guests of honour at a pre-wedding party given for them by Stephen's elder sister, Beatrice, in her beautiful Regent's Park home. In her late forties, she was the wife of a senior civil servant in the Foreign Office. Gabriella had only met her half a dozen times but she liked her, in spite of her formidable manner, which Beatrice had in common with her brother.

Beatrice didn't resemble Stephen physically—she was small and fair and blue-eyed. Stephen said that she took after their mother. His younger sister, Anne, had married a Spaniard and lived in Barcelona—she had been at the party too, but Gabriella hadn't seen much of her. There had been so many people there and she had known only a handful of them—mostly friends of Stephen's whom she had met before.

She had never met his nephew Hugo before; she wished to God that she hadn't met him that night.

'Talk to me,' Paolo said and she started, looking round at him, her face chalky white and her eyes lost and childlike. He drew a sharp breath. 'For heaven's sake! What on earth happened to put that look in your eyes?'

She swayed and he put an arm round her, glancing behind them. 'Come and sit down,' he said, leading her towards a wooden bench at the edge of the hotel gardens. Her legs were trembling so much that she was glad to sit down. She leaned back, closing her eyes.

After a minute she said huskily, 'I realise it sounds stupid, but then I have been stupid with Stephen. I don't really know him. I should never have got engaged, and honestly, Paolo, I don't know how he really feels about me; I can't remember him ever saying he was in love with me.'

Paolo looked incredulously at her. 'Not even when he proposed?'

She shook her head.

From the beginning she had been very ambivalent about Stephen, about their relationship—not sure where it was going or if she should be seeing him at all. When she was with him she was never bored, though; time flashed past, although she could never remember afterwards anything that he had said or anything much that had happened. Looking back on all those evenings with him, she could only remember his face, his grey eyes, his deep voice murmuring.

If he went abroad, and she didn't see him for a week or so, she thought about him all the time. She didn't understand him, yet she couldn't forget him, and although she kept telling herself that she would stop seeing him she never did. When he rang to invite her out she always accepted if she was free, and Stephen knew which nights she worked so he usually made sure to ask her out on her free evenings.

On his thirty-sixth birthday he had taken her to dinner at a very exclusive Mayfair restaurant, whose chef was something of a hero of hers. The food had been marvellous, and she had drunk more wine than usual and felt as if she was floating. Stephen had watched her across the table, his eyes half veiled by heavy lids, and she had been hypnotised by that deep stare, gazing back in sleepy languor while they sipped superb coffee.

'You look lovely in that dress; you should wear white more often,' he'd said.

The compliment had made her flush, and she'd lowered her eyes.

Stephen had stretched a commanding hand across the table and taken her hand, moving his thumb softly up and down against her wrist.

'Gabriella, turning thirty-six has made me stop and think about the way my life is going. I've been too busy building up my business to have time to think of marriage, but since I met you I've realised how much has been missing from my life for years. Living alone isn't natural for human beings—we need each other too much—but I was always so busy that I never had time to see just how lonely I was.'

She had stared, struck dumb. What was he saying? Was he going to ask her to live with him, share his bed, to move into that huge penthouse apartment of his? He couldn't be asking her to marry him!

She had never quite known why he kept seeing her, or what he wanted—and she had been so shy with him that she hadn't dared ask. She had hoped, stupidly, that their relationship would go on in that undemanding, tranquil way.

The moment that he had proposed had been the end of her illusions, although it hadn't dawned on her at once that everything had changed that night. She had been too bewildered.

'I'll be forty in a few years, and the clock is ticking faster. I want a family while I'm young enough to enjoy them,' he had gone on quietly. 'How do you feel about having children? I've noticed you with your cousin's baby; you seem to love looking after him—do you want some of your own?'

Her eyes had glowed. She adored Tommy, her cousin Lara's baby, and she had given Stephen an instinctive, unthinking reply. 'I love children, especially when they're babies; I love to hold them, all milky and smelling of talcum. I envy Lara having Tommy. She says she doesn't want any more—it's too much like work—but I'd like at least four. I was an only child and I was always lonely. I told myself then that I'd make sure that I had more than one child.'

Now she thought, Why did I say all that? I knew what he might be going to say—why didn't I lie, tell him that I didn't want children and he should ask someone else? Why did I babble on like that, misleading him, giving him the wrong impression?

Did I secretly want to marry him? Or was it the same old weakness that has always haunted my life—the inability to recognise danger, to avert catastrophe?

He had picked up her hands and held them loosely, watching the way that her face lit up as she talked about babies, and, when she had finally run out of words and stopped breathlessly, he said, 'Then will you marry me, Gabriella?'

She looked now at Paolo and gave a long sigh. 'I thought he was marrying me because he wanted a family.' That was the truth, wasn't it? Wasn't it?

Paolo's brows shot up. 'Then you realised that you would be sleeping with him?'

She blushed. 'Yes, but . . .' Knowing something with your conscious mind was one thing; realising it at the very deepest level was another. It all depended on how you perceived a situation. Stephen had asked her if she wanted children and she did; she loved the idea of having a baby of her own and finally belonging to a real family again. That had been one aspect of his proposal and their engagement—she had closed her eyes to another aspect of it.

That was why when Stephen had lost control and all that passion had flared out of him she had gone into blinding panic.

If he had acted that way on the night that he had proposed she would have run like hell. But he had been so different then; he had told her softly, 'I'll make you happy, Gabriella!' and she had been lulled into false optimism by that gentleness, the apparent lack of passion. She had drifted into engagement without realising what dangerous waters lay ahead, had let him put his ring on her finger, had let him arrange the wedding, had sat and nodded when he'd made suggestions, had allowed his personal assistant to organise it all, even the invitations to her few friends and family.

The closest of her family were all dead, of course. She only had distant relatives, and her bridesmaids were to have been one of Stephen's nieces and two of her old college friends—and Lara, who was to have been matron of honour in warm peach silk. The rest on the enormous wedding guest list were Stephen's friends and colleagues—some of them wealthy and influential. What would they all be thinking? What would Stephen have told them? Perhaps they would jump to the conclusion that she had run off with another man.

'He suspects you've run off with another man,' Paolo said, as if picking up on her thoughts—as he'd sometimes done in the past, she remembered. They had some sort of mental link; it had always been there, even when they were children. Thoughts flashed from one to the other like electric sparks.

She looked up at him anxiously. 'Did he say so?'

'I picked it up from his voice. *Mia cara*, that is a very jealous man, jealous as hell—I could smell the fire and brimstone down the telephone line!'

She flinched. Yes, Stephen probably did suspect that she had run off with someone. When someone fled from marriage to one man, it was usually to go to another. But jealous? Stephen? Was he? That would be yet another shock discovery, if it was true. I hardly know him at all, she thought; he's as much a mystery to me as he was the day I met him.

'He'll want explanations, answers,' Paolo warned her. 'And you had better have them ready. I have a shrewd idea that he will keep looking for you no matter how long it takes, Gabriella.'

She got up and began to hurry back towards the hotel as if running away again—and that might have been the best plan. Now that Stephen had found Paolo he might hire a private detective to check to see if she was in Como. But there were other places she might go, and he had no idea how close she and Paolo were. Surely he would hunt elsewhere first?

'Will you stay here long?' asked Paolo, reading her mind again, and she shrugged.

'Maybe for the summer. I thought I'd get a job. In a tourist area like this there should be plenty of work available. Do you know anyone with a restaurant or a hotel who needs a chef?'

He shook his head. 'Not offhand, but I'll ask around. I know a few people here who might come up with a suggestion. Come to the villa for lunch.'

'You're a darling, Paolo—another day, thank you. I need to be alone for a while. It helped to talk to you, but I want to take the ferry over to Bellagio and have lunch there; it will give me time to think. I've done far too little of that over the last few months. I want to clear my head and work out what I really do feel.'

'How about dinner tonight, then?'

'I'd love that.'

'Eight o'clock? I'm dying to show you the Villa Caterina Bella. You ought to see it first by daylight, though. The gardens are superb—people come from the other side of the world to see them— and the house itself is a dream—a nineteenth-century fantasy built for a woman who died a few months after it was completed.

'She was the Caterina of the name—a dancer, the mistress of an Italian prince who bought the house for her. He was married to someone of his own class, very respectably, with half a dozen children, when he fell madly in love with a ballet dancer. She was already sick; he hoped that she would regain her health here, by the lake, in the mountain air.

'He made the villa pure paradise for her, but they only had a short time together here before she died of tuberculosis. She's buried in the cemetery here—within sight of the villa and the lake.'

Tears filled her eyes again. 'What a sad story; don't tell me such sad things!'

Paolo looked down at her affectionately. 'Sad but beautiful. Like you! I'll see you tonight at eight, then.'

When he had gone Gabriella went up to her room, collected a light summer jacket, then walked down to the ferry and took the boat across the lake.

She spent the rest of the morning in Bellagio, exploring the shops—some of them hidden away up steep steps—staring at jewellery and leather goods, silk scarves and glass lampshades. She found a hairdressing salon right at the top of the steps; two women were working in it, one dying a customer's hair blonde in streaks, the other just finishing blow-drying another's hair.

Gabriella had her hair washed by a teenager who was learning the business, while she waited for the younger hairdresser to be free. When she told the girl what she wanted the Italian was dumbstruck.

'Cut this?' the girl repeated, running her fingers through Gabriella's long, wet, silky hair. 'You can't be serious? It would be a crime. I wish my hair was this long and looked this good.'

'I'm tired of it; I want it off.' Gabriella lifted her hand to shoulder-length, gesturing. 'Would you cut it in a bob, this long? With a fringe.'

The older hairdresser—a short, plump woman in her forties who probably owned the shop—came over then to plead with her. 'But it suits you long. Believe me, it suits you better the way it is now; you have that sort of face. Long hair is perfect for you.'

'And it will take you years to grow it this long again, you know,' said the younger girl, who wore her own hair in frizzy ringlets which hung right down her back, almost as long as Gabriella's.

'I know, but I'm sick of long hair. I want to change myself,' Gabriella stubbornly insisted. 'I want a complete new look.'

The two women exchanged quick, shrewd looks.

'I hope he's worth it, then,' the older one said, shrugging and walking back to her own customer, who had listened with open curiosity to the discussion.

'No man is!' she called across, looking faintly comic in a space-age foil bonnet with wisps of yellow hair poking through it. 'You'll get over him and then you'll regret having cut your hair off! Don't do it!'

Gabriella looked up at the assistant standing behind her chair. 'I'd like it shoulder-length,' she repeated obstinately, but it made her feel odd to watch the curls of black hair falling to the floor as the scissors snipped and slashed. The teenaged assistant swept it all away a few moments later while Gabriella's now much shorter hair was blow-dried.

She felt strangely light-headed and unfamiliar as she left the shop some time later. Her black hair now swung in a short, graceful bell, the tapered ends shaped to frame her face. She kept catching sight of herself reflected in shop windows, and each time was startled.

She ate lunch at one of the restaurants close to the jetty. From there she could see Menaggio and the cream and gold façade of her own hotel, and could watch the boats coming and going at the jetty. She had managed to get a timetable and had decided to return at around four.

First, having eaten a leisurely, light lunch, she walked further along the waterfront and visited the Villa Serbelloni, which had now been turned into a hotel. The gardens rising in front and behind the great cream-painted building were steep and tiring to explore, but were so beautiful that she spent the rest of the afternoon there, among the towering rhododendrons and camellias, the magnolias and azaleas, their flowers a mass of colours—pink, gold, deep red, orange, violet—a dazzling array. There was a drift of fragrance from roses all around her as she walked, and the busy hum of bees rifling the petals.

Among the shrubs and flowers she found a topiary garden too—sculptured shapes in yew, dark green and secretive, and, rising against the summer sky, the usual cypress, twisting like green flames into the blue air.

She had to hurry to get back to the jetty in time to catch the boat. She had saturated herself in peace and tranquillity and beauty all day; she was pleasantly tired, her mind at rest for a while. She enjoyed leaning on the rail watching Bellagio disappear, and then turning to watch Menaggio coming closer. A delicate opalescent mist had begun to drift along the lake; it gave a new mystery to the distances, the little lakeside villages and towns—they appeared and vanished without warning as if they were fairy places.

When she got to the hotel the receptionist stared, eyes widening. 'Your hair... It's... You've had your lovely long hair cut, *signorina*.'

'That's right,' she said coldly, taking her key, and walked away before he could say what she could feel he was going to say.

Back in her room, she had a bath and changed into one of the new dresses that she had bought for her honeymoon—a heavy cream silk dress, expensively simple in style but a delight to wear because it felt so good on her skin.

Paolo arrived a little early but she was waiting for him downstairs; as she got up and walked towards him he looked at her, then did a double take.

'What on earth . . .? Gabriella, what in the name of the Madonna have you done to yourself?'

Her lower lip stuck out childishly. 'Cut my hair! I was sick of having long hair—it's so much work; it takes so long to wash and dry, and comb, and

brush... I was fed up with it; it's been long for
years. I wanted a change.'

She knew she sounded petulant but she couldn't
help that. Paolo looked at her with his wry smile,
shrugging.

'I see. It was a symbolic act, was it?'

A little defiantly she grimaced at him. 'Don't be
clever with me, Paolo. Shall we go?' She put her
hand through his arm. 'You look stunning, by the
way.'

He was breathtaking—wearing a magnificently
tailored white dinner-jacket, black tie, black
trousers; the combination emphasised his Italian
colouring, his slim figure and his golden tan. Other
women, walking past them on their way to the
dining-room for dinner, stared at him with fasci-
nation and desire but he seemed oblivious of them.

He grinned down at her. 'That's it, get round me
with flattery! I still regret your lovely, lovely hair.
Something else to blame that man for! Come on,
I'm parked outside.'

When they left the hotel she was stunned to dis-
cover that he was driving a Lamborghini—a long,
gleaming white model which was parked right
outside the hotel and being currently admired by
the receptionist, a hotel porter and a couple of the
waiters from the dining-room.

They fell back as she and Paolo appeared; she
recognised the rather supercilious receptionist who
had been so reluctant to let her check in the night
before. He hurriedly smiled and bowed when he
caught her eye. Behind him hovered the boy who
had brought her breakfast. Gabriella smiled at the

boy warmly, pretending not to notice the way he was staring at her new hairstyle. She didn't want him commenting too!

Paolo ceremoniously put her into the passenger seat; the hotel staff watched her long, slender legs swing into place before Paolo closed the door on her.

They drove out of the car park just as another car drove into it, forcing Paolo to slow down. Gabriella glanced at the dark green Jaguar XJS and froze, recognising it. Stephen had a Jag that colour—the colour known as racing green.

Oh, but it must be a coincidence. It couldn't be his car! He wouldn't have had time to get here. Her glance flashed to the number-plate; her heart almost stopped. It was!

Then the driver turned his head, and she couldn't breathe. She slid down in her seat, hoping he couldn't see her.

Paolo was out of the car park a second later and let the throttle out; the Lamborghini shot away along the empty road which was veiled in soft, pearly mist.

He looked sideways as she gripped the edge of the seat, her knuckles white with strain.

'Am I going too fast for you? There isn't much traffic around this evening. I'll slow down if another car shows up, don't worry.'

'It was him,' she said shakily.

'What?' Paolo's brows met.

'Stephen—in the green Jag. It was him.'

Paolo was looking bewildered. 'The green ...' Then his face sharpened in understanding. 'Oh, in the hotel car park? The sports car? Has he got a Jaguar sports? Gabi, you're beginning to be paranoid; don't start seeing him all over the place.'

'I saw his face,' she told him angrily. 'I'm not crazy, Paolo, and I'm not imagining things. I know that car. But how did he get here in it this fast? You said he rang you from London last night.'

'I said he rang me last night; I've no idea where he was ringing from. But he could have come down on the train.'

'No, that is his car, I tell you. I saw the number-plate.'

'Darling, you can put your car on a train.'

She hadn't thought of that. 'Of course you can,' she said, slumping wearily back in her seat. Stephen had found her, tracked her down. For a second she was pole-axed, hopeless, then she sat up with feverish determination.

'I've got to get away, Paolo! I'll have to abandon all my luggage in the hotel, and my car; I can't go back for them—he'll be waiting for me. But I've got my handbag, with my passport and all my money in it. I will have to run again. I'll have to catch a train... Where could I go? On to Switzerland? That isn't far, is it?'

Paolo's gaze was fixed on his driving-mirror, watching the road unwind behind them. He didn't answer.

'Will you help me, Paolo?' she asked and he looked briefly at her, his eyes sober.

'I'm sorry, *cara*, I'm afraid your chances of escape are almost nil—he's right behind us and he's catching up fast.'

CHAPTER THREE

GABRIELLA half turned to look back and saw a flash
of green close behind them. She couldn't see
Stephen through the windscreen of his car but fear
made her nerves leap and her skin prickle. If he
caught up with them . . .

She turned back, breathing in a shallow, rapid
way, cold perspiration breaking out on her
forehead. 'Can't you go any faster, Paolo? Surely
this car must be faster than his! I thought it was a
race-car! You were boasting that it could go up to
a hundred and fifty without even rocking.'

'Not on public roads,' he muttered. 'But I'll do
what I can—although in this mist, on this narrow
road, I don't want to risk going much faster.'

He put his foot down and the Lamborghini
surged forward. She watched the speed indicator
swing wildly upwards and swallowed a knot of
alarm. At any other time she would have been terrified to be in a car travelling at this speed but her
fear of Stephen was more powerful than her fear
of being killed. She threw another look backwards;
the green bonnet was further away now but still
there.

She turned to look at their speed and was aghast
to see the needle on the indicator start to drop. She
cried out in panic, 'Why are you slowing down

again? He's still behind us! Don't slow down, go faster. We've got to get away from him!'

'I'm sorry, *cara*, but there's a narrow bridge up ahead—just room enough for two cars to pass, if they aren't too big. I'm not risking meeting another car head-on in the middle of it!'

The mist seemed much thicker, dense and smoky. She screwed her eyes up to peer into it but couldn't see anything at all.

'I don't see any bridge!'

'It's there—I know this road,' Paolo told her, and at that instant something loomed up in front of them.

Gabriella threw it one, stunned look—it seemed as big as a house, and inexplicable for a second in the drifting swirls of mist. Then she realised what it was, and she screamed, shrinking down in her seat.

'Paolo! Look out!'

The huge shape which had come out of nowhere was a container lorry, driving right over on their side of the road.

Paolo swore under his breath. He'd already had his foot on the brake but now he slammed the brakes full on and the Lamborghini went into a jerky slide, tyres screaming on the wet road while Paolo gripped the steering-wheel tightly, his knuckles turning white.

It all happened so fast yet Gabriella felt that it was all happening in slow motion. She sat there, rigid with terror, as they spun sideways across the road. Paolo was white-faced, with drops of sweat breaking out on his temples, his body flung forwards by the force of the car's braking, his face contorted with fear and intense concentration. The lorry driver had braked too, wrenching his wheel to get himself back on to his own side of the road, but his vehicle moved more slowly, thundering on along the road with the whole weight of it carrying it away from them.

The Lamborghini spun almost in a circle, wheels skidding, and finally came to a stop right up against a stone wall, facing the way they had come. Gabriella heard grinding metal, the car's paintwork being grazed all the way along one side. So did Paolo.

He was swearing. 'Holy Madonna... That's my bloody paintwork! It will cost a fortune to have it re-sprayed; it was perfect, not a scratch on it.'

He undid his seatbelt and threw open his door, scrambled out, then almost fell over as his knees seemed to give under him. He held on to the door, shaking violently. Out of the mist someone came running up to him—a big man, broad and burly, sallow-skinned, unshaven, black-haired, in blue dungarees and a baseball cap.

'*Signore*?' he panted in Italian. 'Are you OK? Are you hurt?'

Paolo groaned. 'I don't seem to be injured, but I'm not OK! My God, I thought that was my last hour!'

'It was the mist—I didn't realise how narrow the road was beyond the bridge. One minute there was nothing in front of me, the next minute there you were. I didn't have time to think; there was no warning.'

Paolo swung round on him, going red with rage. 'Oh, so you're the fool who was driving on my side of the road!'

'No, that's a lie, nothing of the kind! I was just a little over, maybe, but——'

'You nearly killed us, you stupid bastard. Look what you've done to my car—smashed it like a tin can. It will cost a fortune to put right.'

The other man took in the Lamborghini and his face lengthened as he assessed the cost of repairs to a car of that quality. His face reddened in sullen resentment and he glared at Paolo with bulging eyes.

'You were driving too fast, much too fast. I know what a car like this can do! You were driving as if you were on a race-track, in mist like this! No wonder I didn't see you coming; you were probably doing a hundred an hour. You just came at me out of the mist; I didn't have time to get out of your way.'

'Oh, so it's my fault now, is it?' Paolo was shaking with fury, his Italian gestures even more pronounced than usual. 'And it's a lie. I'd slowed right down to take the bridge, and I was on my own side of the road—it was you that was on the wrong side, and don't think you're wriggling out of that, because you're not. The accident was your fault; you aren't blaming me for it. You've already said that you couldn't see a thing because of the mist— and you didn't see me, so how are you going to get away with a claim that I was driving too fast?'

'I heard you!'

'Liar!'

'Who are you calling a liar? Just because you're driving a Lamborghini it doesn't give you the right to call me a liar!'

'I called you a liar because that's what you are!'

Gabriella had been so intent on their quarrel that she had forgotten Stephen for a second, then she caught the flash of headlights right ahead of them, and, glancing forward, saw the green Jaguar being parked into the side of the road close to Paolo's bumper. Then the driver's door opened and Stephen got out, his tall, lean figure sharply outlined in the pale mist.

The shock sent her into instant reaction. She was so terrified that she didn't stop to think. She fumbled with the handle of her door, opened it as far it as far as it would go and got out; she just had enough room to squeeze along the stone wall against which the Lamborghini rested.

Ahead, through the drifting mist, she briefly saw a gleam of light on dark water. That must be the lake, she realised; she could walk back towards her hotel along the lakeside.

She began to run towards the side-road which must lead down to the lake, keeping her head down, hoping that Stephen wouldn't see her. She could hear the fierce argument between Paolo and the lorry driver—they had no attention to spare for her or anybody else—and other cars were there now, slowing, stopping, beginning to sound their horns in protest at being brought to a standstill by the lorry in one direction and the Lamborghini in the other. The noise was deafening; her head ached and she couldn't think.

All Gabriella knew was that she had to get away. She got to the corner and found a narrow lane leading downwards, between small, crammed-together houses which she could barely see in the mist. She began to run flat out down towards the sound of lapping water.

The delicate cream leather high heels that she was wearing were not built for running, especially on slippery wet roads. She skidded several times and had to grab at a wall, but she kept running, her breathing thick and painful in her throat, until she almost hit a wooden railing.

Gabriella caught hold of it to stop herself and leaned there, panting, her chest heaving, listening for the sound of pursuing footsteps. Somewhere in the mist she heard the blare of car horns, raised angry voices, and then the louder wail of a police car coming, but she didn't hear anyone following her down to the lake. Stephen couldn't have seen her running away.

It was so silent down here; the mist deadened all sounds. She stood listening to the soft, hushed lap of water on the jetty which the wooden railings enclosed, the creak of the wooden platform she stood on, a gentle rippling where eddies ran close to the banks, and, further away, a faint quacking from some ducks.

She could see nothing of the other side of the lake; the mist had closed right in. She stared into it, shaking, cold and tense to the point of tears. The accident had been the last straw. She had had to get away.

Suddenly she stopped thinking about herself, realising just what she had done. Paolo. She had deserted Paolo when he was in trouble and needed her. She was his only witness, the only person who could back up his story about the lorry being on his side of the road as it came through the bridge.

She had run to him when she needed help and he'd been there for her. In fact, if it hadn't been for her he wouldn't have been driving this evening, in the mist, far too fast. *She* had urged him to drive faster. *She* had complained when he'd slowed down again.

And then she had run away—run out on him! She should go back. She ought to. She bit down into her lower lip, groaning with guilt and uncertainty. If she went back Stephen would be there...

If she didn't, though, Paolo might be in serious trouble. It would be his word against the lorry driver's.

She closed her eyes for a second, then lifted her head, squaring her shoulders. She had to face it. She had no other choice.

She began to walk back up the hill towards the road; from a distance, through the mist, she saw the police car's flashing light, saw the policeman himself, in a shiny, reflecting yellow mac, sorting out the tangle of traffic, beckoning on a line from one direction while holding back the cars from the other.

Gabriella stopped dead as she emerged on to the main road again. Paolo was standing by his Lamborghini talking to Stephen, who was a head taller, and looked tough and formidable, even though he was wearing one of his dark city suits under a dark overcoat. He was so much more muscular than Paolo. Stephen's shoulders were wider, his body leaner, harder; he managed to make Paolo look lightweight.

As she stood there, trembling, both men glanced round and saw her. She avoided Stephen's eye and looked pleadingly at Paolo; he at once moved towards her, but another police car arrived at that moment, and one of the officers in it came over to question him.

He looked at Gabriella. 'Wait there; this shouldn't take long.'

The policeman looked round at her, asked Paolo a question and got a nod.

Stephen walked towards her with the smooth lope of a predator, his eyes glittering, his face taut and deadly. Her nerves jumped and she began shaking.

Then Paolo called out to her, 'Gabriella, the officer wants to ask you some questions.'

With a gasp of relief, she hurried over to them eagerly—while she was answering the policeman's queries Stephen couldn't get at her. She felt his frustration tangibly even though she avoided catching his eye.

'You were the passenger in the Lamborghini?' the officer asked her in Italian and she nodded.

'Your name, please?'

She gave it and he shot her a sharp look. 'English?'

She explained, got her two passports out of her handbag in the car, showed them to him, told him where she was staying, and gave him her home address in London.

He asked her a series of questions about the accident and she told him that Paolo had slowed right down in anticipation of the bridge and that the lorry had been on their side of the road and going too fast.

'I wanted Paolo to drive faster, but he wouldn't; he's a very careful driver. We had no warning that the lorry was coming; we didn't see its headlights because the bridge obscured our view of the traffic coming from that direction, but suddenly there it was, right in front of us, and so big. It was like driving straight towards a wall. It all happened so fast, too; I still don't know how we avoided hitting him.'

She could see the lorry some way down the road—presumably the first policeman on the scene had dealt with the driver first, to clear the narrow road and make it possible for traffic to flow again. Cars moved past in both directions, skirting Paolo's car which was still parked right into the side of the road.

'Thank you, *signorina*,' said the policeman at last. He turned towards Paolo. 'Now, *signor*, have you got your papers for me?'

Paolo nodded, pulling out his driving licence and a clutch of other documents from the glove compartment of his car.

'Come over to my car; I'll have to use my radio to check these out on the computer,' the policeman said, taking them from him.

Paolo nodded, gave her a quick glance. 'Wait for me in the car—you must be getting cold.' He threw a look at Stephen, waiting a few feet away, and frowned. 'Don't worry,' he told her reassuringly. 'I don't think I'll be long. You'll be OK. If you need me, you only have to yell, remember. The officer and I will be within earshot all the time.'

She knew he was telling her obliquely that she need not be scared of Stephen while he and the police were there.

He walked away with the policeman; they both got into the front of the police car which was parked further up the road and Gabriella went to get into the driver's seat of the Lamborghini, only to find her way barred. She froze, not looking up, staring at the polished black gleam of his shoes.

'Please don't,' she whispered, her voice a mere thread of sound. 'Not now; I've been in a crash. I'm still in a state of shock. I know I'll have to talk to you—try to…explain…but not tonight, please, not tonight. I can't cope with you now.'

Stephen didn't answer. His fingers clamped round her arm, making her wince at the tension she felt in him. Panic leapt in her throat. God, he was so angry! She felt it pulsing and beating inside him.

He began to walk towards his own car, pulling her after him; she fought him, struggling, trying to hang on to the Lamborghini.

'I'll scream… The police are only a few feet away…' She threw a look towards the two parked police cars with their revolving lights making strange circles in the misty air, but nobody was looking towards her and Stephen—they were all too

busy. One policeman was still directing traffic.
Another had walked on through the bridge and was
slowing down traffic coming from the other direction. She saw his swinging yellow lamp as he
moved it, casting flashes of light across the inner
vault of the bridge. The policeman in the car with
Paolo was talking on his car phone; Paolo was too
intent on what was being said to spare a glance for
her.

Wildly she stammered, 'L-Let go of me, Stephen,
or I swear I'll scream the place down. I can't talk
to you tonight; I'll talk to you tomorrow; just let
me go now...'

'With him?' He laughed harshly, without
humour. 'Oh, no, Gabriella. I don't trust you. If
I agreed to wait until tomorrow you would vanish
overnight, with him.'

She was trembling violently. It was flaring out of
him again, that terrifying emotion; it was like facing
the heat and blast of an explosion. She felt her skin
wither and sear, her body shrink.

He pulled open the passenger door of his dark
green Jaguar. 'Get in.'

She was too scared to be able to scream, or even
struggle any more. The force of his emotion had
her in an inexorable grip. Her knees had almost
given way under her; she was boneless and limp as
he shoved her with a peremptory hand into the front
passenger seat of the car, and leant over her to do
up her seatbelt while she sat there numbly, her white
face rigid. The door slammed. He strode round to
get into the driver's seat and still she did not try to
move or call out for Paolo.

She was helpless, trapped in a time warp. It had all happened before; the past rushed back to engulf her.

This was exactly how she had felt on the night of the party—the night before what should have been her wedding-day. Stephen had shattered all her illusions about him when he'd taken her home from his sister Beatrice's party. His cool, controlled manner had cracked apart and underneath she had glimpsed for the first time the real man—the man he had hidden from her all those months; the man she had run from as if from the fires of hell.

She had never met Hugo before. He was Beatrice's eldest son, yet looked more like his uncle—he had inherited Stephen's dark colouring and height, which had originally come from Stephen's father, Gabriella had been told by Beatrice. It was a dominant gene which came out in all the males in that family, Beatrice had said, laughing.

'But skipped me, thank heavens! I prefer to look like my mother. Being blonde has been fun.'

'I've often wished that I were blonde,' Gabriella admitted enviously, but Beatrice looked at her and smiled, shaking her head.

'Darling, you don't need to be blonde. You're very feminine anyway—all that lovely long hair, your beautiful little face, and those gorgeous legs... Why on earth should you need to be a blonde? Don't you agree, Hugo?'

Her son gazed at Gabriella, his eyes gleaming with enjoyment. 'Absolutely! She's perfect just the way she is!'

She blushed slightly, conscious of Stephen listening without expression, his cold face set rigidly.

Hugo worked in New York in an international bank, although you would never have guessed his sedate job from his wild mood during the party. He had obviously come determined to have a good time or was he always like that—laughing, reckless, full of fun? She enjoyed talking to him, but she had to circulate, to meet as many people as possible, because she and Stephen were the guests of honour.

She spent most of the evening talking politely to strangers, most of them much older than she was: friends of the family, business colleagues of Stephen, or friends of Beatrice and her husband. She fought to hide her boredom, kept smiling until her teeth ached and her face felt like concrete; she thought that she had deceived those who did not know her, but when she met Stephen's penetrating eyes she was afraid that he'd realised how she really felt.

The younger people had taken over a large room, turned down the lights, and were dancing in the dark. She couldn't help being a little envious of them. She felt like dancing too. The sensual beat of the music wound into her head and made her body shiver. While Stephen was talking to an influential diplomat, Gabriella took her chance to slip away from a group of people discussing politics, and wandered over to look in at the dancers.

Huge suddenly rushed out of them, grabbed her by the waist and pulled her into the room.

'No, I must go back to Stephen,' she protested, but he just laughed and began dancing with her, both his arms around her, his cheek brushing against hers.

And you let him! she accused herself now. Without trying to stop him, without trying to get away, she had given in weakly, danced with him, her body moving against his with the beat of the music.

He wouldn't let me go! And I couldn't make a scene, could I? I didn't really know what to do so I let him have his own way.

Wasn't that what she always said? 'It isn't my fault. I didn't want it to happen; I didn't know what to do.'

The truth was that she had stood at the door watching the dancers, yearning to be one of them, to move to that deep, hot beat. She had felt it in her bones, in her blood, stirring deep inside her, sensuous and disturbing. She hadn't known exactly what was happening to her, only that she wanted...

Something she couldn't name, wouldn't name.

'Hey! You're good, really good!' Hugo said after a few minutes, looking down at her, his arms tightening round her waist, then he bent his head and kissed her.

It was a light-hearted kiss, warm and laughing, but a second later Stephen was there, pulling her away, his hand cruel on her arm, his face icy.

'Sorry to interrupt when you're having fun,' he bit out, his mouth moving in a cold smile which did not reach his eyes, 'but Sir Henry and his wife are leaving and want to say goodbye to you.'

He didn't even look at Hugo, and his nephew didn't argue. Stephen took her away and Gabriella's nerves were shot to hell for the rest of the evening.

Hadn't she known then that retribution would follow? Even if she hadn't guessed quite what to expect, only known that he was tense with rage— a white-hot rage which made her skin prickle with alarm.

She didn't stray from his side again. She avoided Hugo's eyes, and hardly said a word to anyone unless they spoke to her directly and she had to answer them.

Stephen drove her home. She was relieved to re- alise that he was stone-cold sober. Apart from a glass or two of champagne earlier at supper, he hadn't touched any of the drink which had flowed so freely. She had never seen him drink too much, actually.

He had told her once that when he was young he had gone through a phase of drinking too much and had realised that it was a waste of life. It meant that you slept away half the morning and had a headache for hours next day; it made it hard to do your job. He had realised that he didn't enjoy any- thing about drinking too much. Now he simply en- joyed a glass or two of very good wine with a meal, and maybe a brandy afterwards, but he never went beyond that.

He insisted on walking her to her front door, as he always did, because London was no longer a safe city, he said. Were there any safe cities any- where in the world today? She had to admit that she was relieved that he always saw her into her flat, put on the lights for her and looked into each room before saying goodnight and going.

He never stayed, or tried to—it had surprised her at first. She had waited for it to happen, but it never did. He had never once tried to get her into bed, never asked if he might stay the night. That was one reason why she had let herself relax and trust him, why she had drifted into that engagement, why she had so nearly married him.

That night, though, he did not go with a quiet kiss; he closed the door behind them, and the sound made her stiffen and look at him nervously.

He took off his evening coat and threw it on a chair, staring at her fixedly.

Trembling, she began to back, but not fast enough. He caught hold of her shoulders and pulled her back towards him.

His name was stifled in her throat; she was too alarmed by the way he was looking at her to be able even to scream. She shook her head, though, swallowing, trying to break away while she stared back at him.

His stare was fixed on her mouth; she felt her lips burning as if he were already kissing them. He jerked her off balance until their bodies touched; his body seemed to vibrate against her and she wanted to scream.

One of his hands ran down her body, not simply touching it but possessing it. It was a slow, lingering exploration that made her blood flow hotly every-where he touched—her throat, her shoulders, her breasts, her thighs and inwards. That was when she began to shake from head to foot, when she grew as white as a ghost.

The intimacy was a devastating shock; she drew a long, appalled breath, and Stephen bent his head at that instant, his tongue-tip touching her mouth, tracing the curve of it, sliding between her parted lips. For a second the kiss was so delicate and cool but then it changed, as if someone had thrown a match on to spilt oil. Passion flared in him; he kissed her with such heat and demand that he forced her head backwards, bent her body and fitted his own to it, his chest against her breasts, one of his legs pushing hers apart and moving between them.

She was almost fainting by then. She couldn't breathe with his mouth crushing and bruising hers. She swayed, almost fell, and Stephen pushed her back on to a couch and came down on top of her, the weight of his body holding her captive.

She didn't want to remember the next few minutes; they were illuminated in flashes in her memory—his hand peeling down the bodice of her dress, her bra coming off, his fingers cool on her naked breast, his mouth on her neck, hot and hungry, his mouth sliding down between her breasts, moving on her soft, pale skin, finding her nipples, closing around them and sucking them into his mouth, as if he were her baby.

She was dazed by what was happening, eyes shut tight as if that would make it all stop, as if it would make it less real, her bare skin quivering at the intrusion as his hand slid between her thighs, caressing, arousing, making her burn where he touched, stabbing desire and fear into her body like knives into living flesh.

Tears filled her eyes, trickled into her lashes. She tried to blink them away—could he feel it? Had their salty wetness touched his skin? Or had her tense shivers of fear reached him?

At least—at last—he stopped abruptly, said goodnight, and went. But she realised with terror and sick dismay that that was only the beginning. Once they were married he would not stop, he would not leave; he would stay and go on . . .

I can't! she thought desperately. I just can't bear it. Why did I ever think I could?

Yet the very thought of trying to tell him, to explain, sent those waves of panic through her. She had left it too late. In a few hours she would be his wife and the real nightmare would begin.

So she had run, knowing all the time that Stephen would be behind her, would catch up with her sooner or later.

She had hoped that she would have time to calm down to get the courage to talk to him, to explain . . .

Now she slid a sideways look at his hard face as he started the engine and began to drive away. How could she ever talk to him when he looked like that? She was totally oblivious of Paolo getting out of the police car, running, calling her name.

She was oblivious of everything except the naked fear of knowing that time had run out for her— she had to face Stephen's rage now, ready or not.

CHAPTER FOUR

'WHAT the hell have you done to your hair?' Stephen grated, making her jump.

Gabriella swallowed, and muttered, 'I had it cut yesterday.'

'Why did you do it? Long hair suited you; this doesn't.'

'I like it,' she said defiantly. She wasn't surprised to hear that he didn't—Paolo hadn't liked it either. What was it about long hair on a woman that most men liked so much? Was it because they enjoyed touching it, playing with it, the sensual experience of feeling it slide through their fingers?

Was that why she had had her hair cut? Why *had* she felt that she must do it? She had grown her hair for years. Why, suddenly, had she felt that it had to come off? The question made her uncomfortable. She didn't try to work out the answer. She didn't want to think about it.

'Where are you taking me?' she whispered, but he didn't answer, his gaze fixed on the road and his profile stony. They were driving along the main lake road, not too fast because of the mist and the narrow winding of the road. Where could they be going? Surely to heaven he didn't intend to drive all the way back through Italy and France and across to England? 'Paolo will tell the police...' she began, and he gave a short laugh.

'What?' he bit out. 'That your fiancé has driven off with you?'

She fell silent. Of course Paolo wouldn't say anything to the police, and Stephen was right—what could he say, anyway?

'They would only be interested if I were a stranger,' Stephen added drily and her face tightened even further. A stranger... Wasn't that what he was, though? She had known him for months, but she knew she had barely scraped the surface of the man; they had never talked honestly, with real intimacy; they had never told each other the deep, hidden things about themselves, what they really felt, really thought. They were strangers to each other; he knew as little about her as she did about him.

Stephen shot a look sideways at her, and she felt his tension. 'What are you thinking? That that's what I am—a stranger?'

Gabriella was startled by that—he had read her mind! Paolo often did, but then she and Paolo had grown up together.

'That's what you were thinking, isn't it?' Stephen insisted curtly. 'I read it in your face. You have a give-away face, you know; every feeling you have shows on it. I saw your eyes when I said if I were a stranger, and it was obvious what you were thinking. It's true too—we are almost strangers to each other. It was only when you ran away that I realised how little I knew about you. I had no idea where you might have run off to—and when I asked Lara where you might go she couldn't come up with anywhere either.

'Oh, we both thought of Brindisi, but my people drew a blank there—you weren't staying at any of the hotels, or with any of your distant relatives. Lara couldn't tell me anything about any of your friends; neither could your friends Jilly and Petra. They seemed to me to know very little about you too—not one of them knew anything much about Paolo, for instance. My detectives had to track him down from the Rome address on the wedding-guest list.'

'You hired detectives to look for me?' It was only what she had guessed he might do but she still felt a jolt of shock at the thought of strangers prying into her life, going around asking questions about her, arousing curiosity and gossip.

'I could hardly try to trace you myself—it would have taken me forever to make all the phone calls. We had to check every one of your personal friends, which was when I realised how few really close friends you have. It didn't take long.'

She felt an ache of sadness. No, there were not many people close to her—almost none, really, except Lara and the couple of friends whom she had got to know well in the cordon bleu training-school in London where she had perfected her trade: Jilly, who was working in one of the royal households, a cool ice-blonde with impeccable taste and perfect manners, whose father ran a training stable which frequently trained racehorses for members of the royal family; and Petra, half Russian and explosive in temperament, with flashing dark eyes and spiky black hair, who had gone abroad to work for a chain of exclusive hotels and was currently working in Paris.

Stephen had met them several times—Jilly and Petra were to have been her bridesmaids; they had been at the wedding rehearsal and the party afterwards. She remembered how impressed they had been by Stephen. Jilly hadn't said much—she never did; super-cool Jilly kept her feelings and her thoughts to herself, but Petra had been ecstatic and envious.

'Darling, he's gorgeous. How did you meet him? Has he got a twin brother? I want a guy just like him. Is he very rich?'

'I believe so,' Gabriella had said, laughing because Petra always made her laugh; she had a way of saying things that was irresistibly funny even when she wasn't making jokes.

'Oh, just your luck! Sexy and rich! Whenever I meet a man with enough money he's usually bald, fat and sixty.'

'Gold-digger,' Jilly had said.

Very serious, Petra had shaken her head. 'No, darling, just practical! A girl has to think of her future. Who wants to marry a poor man?'

'If you loved one, would you marry him?' Gabriella had asked and Petra had looked sideways at her, black eyes glinting.

'Don't make my blood run cold! I just try to steer clear of poor men, that's all, especially attractive ones!'

Jilly and Gabriella had looked at each other and laughed, not taking her too seriously. Petra had been falling in and out of love ever since they'd met her, and none of the men had been rich.

Gabriella was fond of both her friends, but she had never confided in them; the friendship was on a very superficial level. That was why she hadn't felt up to ringing them to tell them the wedding was off; she had left it to Lara to warn them, and she felt guilty about that, yet she hadn't been able to face the questions they were bound to ask.

'Did you talk to Jilly and Petra yourself?' she whispered.

'Yes. They seemed genuinely taken aback. You hadn't talked to them, had you? They couldn't— or wouldn't—tell me anything I didn't already know. I asked them about Paolo and drew a blank there too. They claimed they'd never heard of him.'

'I don't suppose they have. He has only been to England once—I hadn't even left school then. I didn't know them then and I doubt if I've ever mentioned him to them.'

Stephen was silent, staring out into the veils of mist which kept blowing across the road. Gabriella suddenly realised that the car had slowed right down, was crawling along. If he drove much slower she would be able to open her door and jump out, she thought, her muscles tensing at the idea. What if she got hurt when she fell, though? And if she landed without injury, what would she do then? Run away in a strange town in damp lake mist? Where to?

She wasn't wearing a coat, just a thin silk dress, and impractical high heels, and a fine drizzle was falling in the mist. She would be soaked within

minutes. And even if she did run, where would she
go? Wasn't that why she had gone back to the scene
of the accident a short time ago? Because she had
nowhere to run to anyway?

No, that wasn't true! She had gone back because
she hadn't been able to desert Paolo when he'd
needed her to be a witness for him; it had been
selfish and cowardly to run out on him when he
was in trouble. Paolo would never have done that
to her.

Her face quivered. OK, maybe that was one
reason why she had gone back—but even if Paolo
hadn't needed her, where could she have gone? To
the hotel? Or to the villa where Paolo was staying?
Stephen would have found her again immediately.
A shudder went through her. She couldn't hide from
him. She had known that from the minute she had
begun to run. She had sensed him on her trail, had
been afraid he would find her, wherever she went.

She knew that much about him. He was re-
lentless, tenacious, insistent—a man who wouldn't
give up anything without a fight.

He suddenly wrenched the wheel and the car
slewed across the road, making her start violently,
her nerves leaping. For a second she thought there
was going to be another accident, but there was no
other car in sight.

'Where are we going?' she broke out, trembling.

Ahead of them through the mist she just saw
high, intricate wrought-iron gates—they had turned
off the road on to a driveway. Stephen held something in his hand, pointed it, and the gates began
to swing open as they drove towards them.

'Is this a hotel?'

Stephen still didn't answer. They were through the gates, which closed again behind them. She was sitting forward, tensely trying to see through the mist. Lights shone somewhere in the distance. She prayed that it was a hotel—if he had brought her somewhere so public then she was safe; she needn't be afraid what he might do.

Faintly she glimpsed high stone walls rising on the right-hand side of the car. On top of the walls was some sort of wiring—were they electrified?

Following her gaze, Stephen said quietly, 'Yes, the whole perimeter of the grounds is electrified. Nobody gets in, nobody gets out.'

'Is it a hotel?' she repeated, her hands twisting in her lap. Please, please, let it be a hotel, she begged silently.

'No, it's a private villa,' he said drily, watching her hands clench together. 'It belongs to a friend who's in Florida—she's lent it to me for a few days.'

'She?' She was startled into repeating the word, her blue eyes lifting to his face.

'The widow of an old friend,' he expanded, his gaze narrowed and searching. 'Kay has put the villa on the market; she lived here with her husband until he had a heart attack and died within minutes. She's an American, and without George she was lonely here; she wanted to go home, so she bought a villa in Florida, one of my developments. Her place is set in a large garden, with a big swimming-pool, but it is much easier to run than this villa, which needs a whole team of servants.'

Gabriella was staring at the lighted windows of the villa as they slowly pulled up in front of a double flight of stone steps leading up to the entrance. The mist made it impossible to see much of the building, except that it was of a classical design, and probably at least early nineteenth century, with rows of flat windows on either side of the columned entrance.

She glimpsed palest creamy yellow paint on the stucco walls, and white roses growing entwined along the balustrade of the steps, ghost-like and shimmering, their fragrance still hanging in the air even though the sun had sunk behind the mountains long ago.

'Is there anyone else here?' she asked nervously as Stephen turned off the engine.

'A skeleton staff of servants.' He opened his door and got out, and walked round to open her door.

She didn't move, hunched and tense in her seat.

'We can't talk sitting in the car,' Stephen coldly pointed out.

'Why not?' she whispered, and heard his impatient movement.

'Oh, for God's sake—what are you afraid of? That I may turn violent? I give you my word I won't. You walked out on our wedding on the very day itself without doing me the courtesy of explaining to my face why you felt you couldn't go through with it. I think I'm owed that explanation, Gabriella. Don't you?'

A sigh went through her. How could she deny it? Yet how could she bear to tell him anything that would explain?

He reached into the car and hooked an arm around her waist. 'Come on, Gabriella. Get out.'

The feel of his warm hand right under her breast made a wild tremor run through her whole body.

'OK!' she broke out hoarsely, trying not to betray herself by trembling. 'OK, I'll get out. Let go of me! I don't need any help.'

He released her without comment, holding the door open as she swung her legs sideways, put her feet down on the gravelled drive, got out and stood up, the top of her head coming somewhere around his chin, reminding her of how much taller he was, and how much more powerful. If he chose to exert his male strength she would have no chance whatever in fighting him, but her fear of him was not based on his physical superiority.

She wasn't afraid that Stephen might hurt her, not deliberately, not knowingly. He simply wasn't the type to hit a woman, perhaps because he was such a big man and so aware of his own strength. It was men who were aware of their weakness, men who had an inferiority complex, who wanted to hurt women, to take their revenge for their own failures.

He put a hand under her elbow to guide her, but his touch was light and cool.

'This way,' he murmured, steering her to the foot of one side of the dual staircase.

She shot a look at the top of it and realised that the front door, which had been closed, now stood open; a wide band of yellow light from within spilt out on to the stone steps. Gabriella began to climb, with Stephen keeping step with her.

They had almost reached the top when she became conscious of a man standing above, watching them. He was wearing a black jacket and trousers and a green and yellow striped waistcoat over a white, ruffled shirt. It was clearly some sort of uniform—was this one of the servants?

When they reached the top of the steps he bowed from the waist, saying something in Italian; she didn't catch the words but Stephen answered in Italian. She had known that he spoke several languages, including Italian, but he had only once used her childhood language to her, when he had first heard that she had grown up in Brindisi. Usually they spoke to each other in English and it seemed strange to hear him casually speaking Italian now.

'This is Adriano,' he told her. 'He is in charge of the house while Signora Adams is not here. Adriano, this is my fiancée, Signorina Brooks.'

Adriano bowed again. He had sleek black hair which was receding slightly at the temples and showing faint streaks of silver here and there. His thin, sallow face was very brown and wrinkled; he could have been any age from forty to sixty, but she had a suspicion that he was much older than he looked.

'Supper is laid, as you ordered, in the small supper-room,' he said, and this time his Italian was clear; she understood every word. He spoke with the local accent, she realised then. He must have been born in this region of Italy, which explained why she hadn't understood him at first—it had taken time for her ear to become tuned to his accent.

What he had said sank in slowly, though. Supper? Had Stephen been so sure that he would be bringing her back here?

'May I show the *signorina* to a room, to wash her hands before supper?' Adriano asked, and Stephen glanced at her, silently raising his brows in query.

'Yes, please,' she said, needing a few minutes alone to pull herself together.

Adriano waved his hand at the open front door. '*Per favore, signorina.*'

He stood back and she slowly walked into the villa, her eyes skating hurriedly around the large hall in which she found herself; it took her breath away as she saw the towering white columns rising up to support a white and gold ceiling lit with glittering chandeliers.

The marble floor was partly covered by a blue and gold carpet—squares of blue set with a formal spray of gold flowers, each square surrounded by a band of classical gold design. The blue was picked up again in floor-length blue velvet curtains, both blue and gold repeated in the nineteenth-century hall chairs arranged at intervals along the length of the hall—gilded wood, blue satin brocade seats.

Halfway along the hall a flight of stairs rose up to the first floor, carpeted with the same design.

Adriano bowed her towards them. 'This way, *per favore, signorina.*'

Stephen said quietly, 'Don't take too long, will you?' and walked away down the hall; she saw him vanish through an open door.

The first floor held rows of doors; Adriano showed her to one of them and waved her inside the room. It was a luxuriously furnished bedroom—rose-pink and cream, with a four-poster bed, with carved posts at each corner and a pink velvet canopy above it, a pink and cream carpet, pale cream-painted walls, an ornately gilt-framed mirror, on each side of which were gold-painted candle-holders.

Adriano trod softly across the carpet, opened a door on the far side of the room and gestured politely. 'The bathroom, *signorina*. Would you like me to wait for you——?'

'I'll find my own way back downstairs,' she interrupted, and he bowed again.

'Of course. Excuse me, *signorina*.'

He went out, closing the door behind him, and Gabriella felt the terrible tension leak out of her. She was alone, for a moment or two. She walked into the bathroom and closed the door, locked it and stared blankly around the room.

It was furnished in the Victorian style. It looked original, not reproduction; it had that solid feel to it, the walls fully tiled in white and black in a diamond pattern, the bath huge, wide and deep enough almost to drown in, sheathed in a case of heavy mahogany with a high polish, the inside white enamel, with elaborate gold taps, above which, on the wall, was coiled a very old-fashioned hand-held shower.

Gabriella sat down on the cork-topped bathroom stool. In the mirror on one wall she saw her pale face, her eyes huge, pupils enormous, her black lashes damp and sticking together as if she had been crying. But she hadn't, had she?

Maybe her lashes were damp from the mist she had run through down to the lake? She brushed a hand across them, angry with herself. She had to get herself under control. She had to explain to Stephen, to tell him why she had walked out on their wedding-day, and it was going to be one of the hardest things she had ever had to do in her life.

Her eyes met their reflection again, and there was anguish in them. Not the hardest, of course.

She wouldn't think about that now. She needed all her courage to face Stephen; she couldn't use it up in thinking about the past.

She got up, shivering, used the lavatory, and washed her hands and face in the solid white enamelled basin, grateful for the touch of cool water on her skin. She particularly splashed water on her eyes for some time; after that she felt a little better.

She combed her hair back into shape, renewed her make-up, inspected herself from head to foot—she looked normal enough. How was it possible to look so ordinary when what was happening inside you was cataclysmic?

Well, she couldn't stay in here forever. Sighing, she unlocked the door and went back down the stairs. Adriano was waiting at the foot of them; he gave her one of his bows, plus a polite smile—she detected no touch of curiosity in his eyes. But then as he didn't work for Stephen he had no idea what this was all about; why should he be curious?

'Please follow me, *signorina*,' he murmured in his local Italian, and she obeyed, her legs unsteady as she walked along the wide strip of blue and gold carpet, staring at paintings on the wall, gold-framed canvases which she thought had an eighteenth-century look—large, bosomy women in satin and sallow-skinned men in dark suits staring out with arrogant self-confidence, behind them Italianate backgrounds—hills and trees and ruined castles.

'Are those family portraits?' she asked Adriano, who glanced up at them indifferently.

'They have always hung there, *signorina*; they are portraits of the ancestors of the man who built the villa, an Italian manufacturer from Milan, but he had no children so the portraits were sold with the villa when he died. Some people say the portraits weren't even genuine—he had had them painted to invent a family background for himself. He was a self-made man, from the back streets of Milan. He had made a fortune and dreamt of starting a dynasty. When his first wife, whom he blamed for being barren, died, he hurriedly married a second wife, almost half his age, but she had no children either, so it must have been him who couldn't father a child.'

'How sad.'

Adriano shrugged and threw open a door, bowing her through it. She stopped on the threshold, staring at a small table in the centre of the shadowy room, at the soft gleam of candlelight on silver and crystal, a bottle of wine in a silver wine-cooler, at Stephen standing by a massive stone fireplace, one polished shoe on a brass hearth-surround, watching a log fire sending flames leaping up the blackened chimney. He turned to look towards her, but it was to Adriano that he spoke.

'I'll ring if I need you. Thank you.'

Adriano bowed, and silently closed the door.

'Don't just stand there, Gabriella; come and sit down,' Stephen added drily, moving away from the fireplace to the table. He pulled back a chair for her and she sank on to it, glad to sit down because her knees were shaking. Stephen took her white damask napkin and flicked it open, laying it across her knees.

In front of her stood a large silver dish filled with crushed ice not yet beginning to melt, into which had been pushed down a crystal bowl containing half a melon, hollowed out and then refilled with prawns and strawberries and small balls of yellowy-greeny melon.

'A glass of white wine?' Stephen had picked up the bottle from the wine-cooler and was holding it over one of the glasses arrayed in front of her.

'Thank you.' She watched the clear golden wine fall in a stream into her glass. She almost never drank, but suddenly she needed something to dull her senses, an anodyne, to make it easier for her to talk to him and give him the answers he was going to insist on. She picked up the glass and sipped; the wine was crisp and dry on her tongue.

It gave her the courage to blurt out, 'Paolo is going to be worried. I should get in touch with him to tell him where I am and——'

'I rang the villa where he's staying and left a message,' Stephen said curtly. 'Forget about him for the moment—eat your melon.'

She took a spoonful of fruit; it was very chilled. She ate it slowly, staring as if hypnotised at the double-branched candelabra in the centre of the table; the candles burnt with a flickering light.

'Is this too cold for you?' asked Stephen, and she shook her head and drank some more wine.

'How did you get here?' he asked and she gave him a startled look.

'I drove.'

'All the way from the Channel?' His black brows rose in sardonic disbelief. 'Why didn't you take the TGV to Nice and drive on from there? It would have halved the time you took, and made it a much less exhausting trip. You could have slept overnight in a cabin, had breakfast while they got your car off the train and felt quite fresh for the rest of the journey.'

'Is that what you did?'

'Of course. I did consider flying, but I dislike hired cars.'

They had both finished their melon so he got up and removed the silver dishes, placing them on a trolley waiting discreetly on the other side of the room. He brought back from it two plates which held chicken masked in a smooth, cold, creamy sauce. After that he produced a large bowl of mixed salad and a bowl of hot new potatoes decorated with sprigs of mint and tossed in butter.

'Can I help you to salad and potatoes?'

'I'll do it, thank you—can I give you some?' she said, picking up the salad servers.

'A little of each, thank you.' He refilled her glass while she was piling some salad and several small golden potatoes on to his plate. 'That's perfect, thanks,' he said.

It was all so polite and remote, as if they had never met before. Gabriella wanted to scream. What was he waiting for? When was he going to start the inquisition? She knew now how it felt to be stretched on the rack; she was in agony before he had even asked a single question.

He shifted in his chair and she started, her nervous gaze flying to his face. His brows met; he looked at her angrily.

'Stop it!'

'What?' she whispered, white-lipped.

'Jumping every time I so much as breathe! What on earth do you think I'm going to do to you?'

She looked down at the food on her plate, swallowing convulsively on a wave of sickness.

'I... Nothing; of course I don't... I...' Her stammering died away and was succeeded by silence.

Stephen watched her. 'Tell me about Paolo.'

It was going to begin now. She took a breath to steady her voice. 'He's a painter, a set-designer for TV and the theatre. He lived next door to me when I was a child, in Brindisi. His mother was my mother's best friend, until she died... my mother, I mean... and we left, my father and I, for England.'

'But you kept in touch with Paolo?'

'We wrote and exchanged Christmas cards.'

'He's older than you, obviously.'

'Yes. By four years.'

'Have you seen him again since your mother died and your father took you back to England?'

The questions came tersely, in a cool, clipped voice; she answered them more slowly, huskily.

'Yes, I told you—he came to England while I was in my last year at school.'

'How long did he stay?'

'Only two weeks.'

'How old were you?'

'Seventeen.'

Stephen drank some more wine, his frowning stare fixed on the candle-flame; she risked a glance at him and saw the flame reflected in his eyes, making them glitter and shine with fire. Gabriella shivered. His gaze flicked to her face then and she hurriedly looked away, a pulse beating in her neck.

'You're in love with him,' Stephen curtly accused, and she stiffened, shaken.

'No! Of course not. He's my friend, that's all.'

His eyes bored into her. 'Yet when you ran away from me it was to him!'

She answered before she thought how to choose her words. 'Because I trust him!'

Stephen went rigid, turned white then dark red. 'What have I ever done to you to make you think you can't trust me?' His voice was bitter and stung like a whip.

She was frozen, her eyes wide and terrified, filled with shifting emotions; Stephen stared into them, his mouth hardening.

'This is about what happened after my sister's party, isn't it?' he said harshly, and her eyes answered for her. His frown deepened, his voice roughened, hurrying out the questions as if his patience had run out. 'You're going to have to tell me sooner or later, Gabriella. Is it just me who turns you off—or are you scared of sex? Did something happen to you? Someone hurt you some time? Tell me about it, for God's sake; don't just sit there staring, like a rabbit in a snare. You're not making a sound but I can almost hear you screaming. My God, Gabriella, I'm not a monster—do you think I want to feel you shrinking and trying not to faint every time I touch you?'

CHAPTER FIVE

'I'M SORRY,' Gabriella whispered, filled with guilt at what she had done to him. She had never meant to hurt or harm him. She hadn't thought he would care so much. After all, he had never once said that he loved her. Stephen's proposal had been more like a business proposition—a suggestion for a merger, practical, down-to-earth, full of common sense. He had more or less said it would suit them both, give them both what they wanted—him a settled home life with children, her stability, a family again.

All the same, she should have remembered that he was human. He might be a man with a powerful drive—in fact she had never met anyone with such energy and fixed determination—but he was still human; he was not a machine or a robot. He needed that fierce self-confidence of his to keep him ahead. Anything that undermined his confidence would damage his image of himself, and interfere with his ability to work. Gabriella didn't know much about men, but one thing she had been taught long ago, and which was indelibly printed on her mind, was that however strong a man seemed on the outside he could be destroyed by his own feelings; he could not bear rejection or humiliation.

She looked at Stephen with blue eyes clouding with tears that almost blinded her. 'It—it isn't you,' she stammered. 'It's nothing to do with you... Oh, it's such a mess, and it's all my fault. I'm sorry; I never meant this to happen...'

She pushed her chair back and blundered across the room, only to collide with a small table on which stood a silk-shaded lamp with a finely embossed glass base. The table crashed over, and with a noise like an explosion the glass base of the lamp shattered into dozens of glittering pieces.

Gabriella stood stock-still, staring down at them, horrified. It was somehow the last straw, that stupid, pointless destruction. Was that all she could ever do—hurt people, wreck things, destroy? 'Oh, no, your beautiful lamp...I'm sorry, I'm sorry,' she groaned, getting down on her hands and knees, and began frantically trying to pick up the pieces.

The shards of glass were dagger-sharp but she was so distraught that she didn't even feel it when she cut herself, or notice the blood welling out of her skin.

'What the hell do you think you're doing?' Stephen said fiercely from above her a moment later, grabbing her by the shoulders and hauling her to her feet. 'Leave it! I'll get Adriano to pick it up!' Then he took hold of her wrist, lifted her hand, and broke out angrily, 'You've cut your hand open—look at it!'

She looked at the bright red blood seeping through her skin and swayed, paper-white.

He made a rough, angry sound in his throat—a growl of rage—then suddenly she found herself being lifted off the ground, his arm around her waist, another hand under her knees. Alarmed, she clutched at him with the hand that wasn't injured, fingers closing on his shirt; she gave a frightened glance upwards, into eyes that glittered like the dagger-points of glass on which she had impaled herself.

'What are you doing?'

'That hand needs medical attention,' he bit out, still sounding very angry, 'and you looked as if you were about to faint.'

'No... I...I'll be fine... Put me down, please...'

He ignored that, strode across the room with her, shifted her weight to free one hand so as to open the door and then paused as he came face to face with Adriano, who looked at them impassively, as if not surprised to see Stephen carrying her.

Had he been listening at the door? Gabriella dazedly wondered. She was feeling very odd, light-headed. Maybe Stephen was right; maybe she was a little faint.

'Is there a first-aid box anywhere?' Stephen coolly asked Adriano, without putting her down. 'There has been an accident—one of the lamps has been broken, I'm afraid—and the *signorina* has cut her hand on a piece of glass.'

Adriano's glance went to her injured hand hanging down beside her, then he looked past them into the room to assess the damage. He didn't comment, but merely said, 'I will bring you the first-aid box, *signor*.'

'I'm taking the *signorina* upstairs. She must have the hand washed before I dress it—there could be pieces of glass embedded in the skin; I may have to use tweezers to get them out, and a magnifying glass to make sure I don't leave any tiny fragments behind.'

'Perhaps I should try to get hold of a doctor, *signor*?'

'First I'll see what I can do. It may be necessary to call a doctor if I can't get all the glass out.' Stephen shot a look over his shoulder at the table laid with their food. 'Oh, and when you've brought me the first-aid box clear all that food away, Adriano—we won't be eating any more. You can make some strong coffee later, when the *signorina* is feeling better.'

He walked away along the hall. Aware of Adriano watching them, Gabriella couldn't struggle or try to get down. She waited until the other man vanished from sight. Her head was near Stephen's chest; she could hear his heart beating, a deep, resonant echo of her own, hear his thickened breathing, feel the warmth of his body under his shirt. He was too close; she was too aware of him. She had to get away, but she couldn't embarrass him with the other man staring at them—Stephen would hate it if she did. She had humiliated him enough.

I'm a disaster, she thought miserably, I do nothing but smash things, hurt people, make a mess of my own life and everyone else's. Oh, God, I wish I were dead.

And then she felt a strange, angry surge inside her, a feeling she had had before, had forced down out of sight many times, because she knew she had no right to feel rage or resentment—she was the one who was guilty; she was the one to blame. The feeling was stronger this time; she couldn't push it down, deny it—the rage was making her head pound, her skin burn.

As Stephen reached the foot of the stairs she burst out, 'Put me down! I can walk; I've only cut my hand; I'm not a cripple!'

He looked down at her, frowning grimly. Her face had flushed, turned dark red; her eyes were feverish with anger.

'Put me down!' she repeated hoarsely, and that time he obeyed, lowering her until her feet touched the ground. But his stare darkened, fixed on her face. Stephen was angry too. Rage flashed between them like summer lighting across meadows. His hands clenched at his sides; his skin ran with dark colour.

Gabriella was frightened for a second, then she lifted her chin in a gesture of defiance. 'Now please get me a taxi; I want to go back to my hotel.'

His mouth barely parted to bite out his answer. 'Not until I've dressed that hand.'

'I'll have it done at the hotel!'

'You'll have it done here,' Stephen said brusquely. 'Upstairs, in a bathroom—it must be washed and any glass fragments taken out before it is bandaged.'

She opened her mouth and he put his hand over it.

'Don't argue, Gabriella! Either you let me do your hand or we call a doctor. Which is it to be?'

She raged helplessly, her eyes seething over that muzzling hand. She didn't want a doctor; he would ask questions, be curious. No, she had no choice, had she?

'Very well,' she accepted, with resignation. 'You do it—but when you've finished I want that taxi, please! I am going back to my hotel.'

She began to climb the stairs, wishing that her legs wouldn't tremble so much under her. Stephen stayed a stair behind her and once, when she almost missed her step, she felt him put out a hand to catch her. She stiffened and hurried on upwards.

At the landing he caught up with her and said curtly, gesturing to the room she had used earlier, 'We'll use the bathroom in there.'

Wordlessly, she walked into the bedroom and through it to the bathroom. Stephen pulled a cork-topped stool out for her to sit on beside the basin. He held her hand under lukewarm, running water to wash away the blood, then gently dabbed the site of the wound dry with some cotton wool from a large glass jar.

Adriano arrived a moment later with a large first-aid box with a big red cross on the lid. He held a magnifying glass and a pair of tweezers.

'If there anything else I can do, *signor*?' he asked, lingering, staring at Gabriella's palm.

Stephen shook his head. 'No, thanks, Adriano—except make that coffee. We'll want it in about fifteen minutes.'

When Adriano had gone Stephen spread her hand out on the edge of the basin and stared at the palm through the magnifying glass, frowning.

'Keep absolutely still! This may hurt a little, but try not to jerk your hand away.'

She shut her eyes, tensing; the fear of pain was worse than pain itself, she thought wryly. She felt the cold, metallic touch of the tweezers and a faint stabbing as Stephen pulled a piece of glass out of the wound. She held herself still, not making a sound. He extracted several other fragments.

'The tweezers are too clumsy; I'm going to have to use a needle,' he said a moment later. 'You're being very good. I'm sorry if I'm hurting, and it may hurt even more when I use the needle, but I'll be as careful as I can.'

He sterilised the needle by putting the point of it into disinfectant for some moments. Gabriella opened her eyes to look at her palm; the blood was still welling up slightly but it wasn't bleeding as much as it had been.

'Ready?' Stephen asked gently, taking the needle out of the disinfectant.

She nodded, shutting her eyes again. He was quite right—the needle did hurt more; she felt the fine point of it probing her torn and tender flesh and had to bite down on her inner lip to stop herself crying out. It was a terrible relief when he finished, and washed her hand again under the tap. He took a final look at it through the magnifying glass.

'I think I've got it all out,' he said quietly. 'But there may be an odd tiny piece I can't see; don't you think you ought to go to a hospital casualty department to have the hand X-rayed, to make quite sure?'

'No, I'll be OK.'

'Why are you so obstinate?' he muttered, then carefully cleaned her wound again with a mixture of disinfectant and water before drying it and bandaging it.

Now that he had finished Gabriella was released from her tension; she relaxed, trembling, and Stephen gave her a sharp look.

'You aren't going to faint, are you? You're very pale.' His arm went round her, lifting her before she knew what he meant to do; he carried her out to the bedroom and laid her on the bed, then turned away to pick up the phone.

She was too shaken to protest or try to sit up again. She was incredibly tired; she shut her eyes and lay still, listening to Stephen's deep, curt voice.

'Adriano, is the coffee ready? Good, then bring it up here, please.'

He put the phone down; she felt him watching her but he didn't say anything, or come any closer. He began to walk around the room; she didn't risk a look at him; she just heard him, felt him—walking across the room and back, over and over again, with a soft pacing that made her want to scream. It was like the restless, impatient lope of an animal in a cage longing to get out.

Adriano came a moment later, carrying a tray which he placed on a table near the window. She heard the rattle of the cups, the chink of a spoon.

'Thank you. I'll pour it, Adriano,' Stephen said.

'*Sì, signor*,' the Italian said, and walked out again quietly, closing the door behind him.

Panic fluttered in Gabriella's throat as it dawned on her that she was alone in a bedroom with Stephen. She heard the chink of the coffee-pot on a cup. He came over to the bed a moment later.

'Sit up and drink your coffee.'

Shakily she obeyed, resenting the terse voice. Did he have to keep talking to her as if she were a criminal? She put out her uninjured hand to take the cup and saucer, then frowned, looking at the creamy white coffee he had poured her.

'Oh . . . I wanted it black. I never take cream in my coffee—too many calories.'

'This is no time for dieting,' he snapped, going back to the table to get his own coffee.

She seethed, but didn't have the energy to make a fuss over it. She took a sip and made a face at the taste. 'It's sweet!'

'You need to raise your blood sugar,' he told her, coming back towards the bed, carrying his cup and saucer. He sat down on the edge, and her throat fluttered with panic. To cover it, she drank some more coffee while Stephen lifted his own cup to his lips.

She risked a glance at him and was even more alarmed to see the strong, dark planes of his face set in a remorseless insistence. She had hoped to get away without having to explain anything but one look at that face and she knew he wasn't going to let her leave until he had answers. She had thought of him a few moments ago as a caged animal, but it was she who was trapped. She had no hope at all of escaping from this house, from these grounds, from this man.

Shivering, she drank the rest of her coffee and as she finished it Stephen took the cup out of her hands and put it down, beside his own empty one, on a bedside table.

Hurriedly, she moved to get off the bed. 'I'd like to go now, please.'

Stephen grabbed her shoulders and held her, his fingers biting into her. 'You know I'm not letting you leave until you tell me why you ran out on our wedding.'

He didn't shout, but his voice was barely controlled; she heard the anger beneath the quiet surface of it and froze, rigid, unable to move.

She swallowed, her throat dry and painful, and whispered, 'I... You...' She stopped, and tried again, even more huskily. 'That night, that last night, after the party, I realised I couldn't go through with it. I just can't marry you. I thought I could, but I can't. I'm sorry, I know you're angry; it was a rotten thing to do to you, and I'm sorry, but I really couldn't help myself. It was all a terrible mistake; I should never have let it go ahead.'

She heard his breathing, rough, irregular, felt the tension in the hands still holding her, and her nerves went crazy again. It was like being on the edge of a volcano—any minute now, she kept thinking, any minute now, it is going to blow sky-high, and take me with it.

'You still haven't told me why,' he said. 'Tell me about what happened to you.'

'Nothing happened, nothing at all!'

'It must have done, Gabriella!' he broke out, his voice harsh. 'Don't lie to me. Do you think I'm not aware of what happens inside you every time I come too close? Either you're terrified of me or you're terrified of every man you meet; it didn't take me long to realise you were scared stiff of being touched.

'Why do you think I've kept my distance all these months, while we were engaged? Why do you think I gave you a little peck on the cheek now and then, held your hand . . . acted as if we were teenagers instead of adults?' His tone turned angrily sardonic, his grey eyes flashed. 'Or were you under the impression that I was totally sexless? That I wasn't going to make any demands on you after we were married? Did you think I was some sort of eunuch?'

She looked helplessly at him, then gave in and told him the unvarnished truth. 'I was living like a sleep walker; I was trying not to think at all. I knew, of course, that it was madness, that I couldn't marry you, but you seemed so calm and in control. You never——' She broke off, shivering. 'I let myself be hoodwinked into thinking that maybe . . . maybe it would be OK, maybe it would work out.'

He repeated slowly, '"Calm and in control"?' His mouth twisted with a sombre, self-mocking sarcasm. 'Is that what you thought? Oh, I had myself on a leash OK. I didn't know what exactly the problem was, but I knew there was some sort of problem with you, and I tried hard not to frighten you. And then I lost control the night after the party—that was what scared you into running away, wasn't it? That I lost control?'

She looked down, her lashes dark on her pale skin, her mouth bloodless and quivering, and couldn't get a word out; if she said anything it might be too betraying; she might say too much.

Stephen put a hand against her face and she tensed at once, looking back at him hurriedly, with alarm.

His eyes were molten, the grey glittering, the black pupils enlarged and glistening with desire. She drew a rough breath, burst out, 'Don't!' and shoved him hurriedly away with both hands.

Stephen made a rough sound in his throat and grabbed her again, yanking her violently towards him.

'Don't push me away! Don't ever push me away again!'

Gabriella arched away from him, giving a cry of alarm, shaking her head, but as her lips parted to protest his mouth crushed down against them in fierce demand, and although all the alarm bells went off inside her again the passion in his mouth made heat begin to burn deep inside her.

He pushed her backwards, off balance; she instinctively clung to him, trying to stay upright, but his body pressed her down on to the bed. He fell on top of her, and her senses went crazy. She loved the feel of his mouth, his exploring hands as they roved from her throat down to her warm breast and the soft female curve of her body. She couldn't stifle the moan of pleasure in her throat; she wanted what he was doing to her. Sensuality beat in her, made her body quiver and her blood run hot.

His lips slid down her throat. Her ears drummed with the sound of her own blood, deafening her, making it almost impossible to think. She was deeply aware of his body lying against her, hard and masculine; every nerve in her was sensitive to him, every cell in her body clamoured for closer contact with his, and she had always felt this hungry response. It had never disturbed her; it was purely physical; it could not destroy the way emotion could.

If only it could be just their bodies moving together in this passionate languor; if only they could keep their hearts and minds silent forever.

Stephen slowly lifted his head, his eyes, half hidden by heavy lids, moving over her yielding body. Gabriella stared back at him, breathing quickly, her heart beating fast.

'Now tell me you didn't enjoy that,' he said, his voice husky, triumphant, rough with desire.

She trembled, couldn't answer, feeling the need aching inside her. He could have gone on without meeting any resistance—he could have taken her and she would not have tried to stop him. She had never been scared by the idea of going to bed with him.

Stephen's grey eyes probed her face, the parted, trembling curve of her pink mouth, still swollen from his kisses, the wide, darkened blue eyes.

Slowly he said, 'So it isn't being touched that scares you. You aren't scared now, are you? What is it, Gabriella? What sent you into panic that night? What was different that time?'

She shut her eyes and forced herself to say the truth. 'You,' she whispered.

'Me?' A silence. Then he asked, 'How?'

'You were...' She couldn't finish the sentence and stopped dead, her mouth full of the taste of ashes, the memory of anguish.

He waited for a moment, then quietly finished it for her.

'Out of control? Is that what you were going to say?'

She was still unable to speak, her memory haunted by moments she had spent years trying to forget.

Quietly Stephen asked her, 'Somebody once lost control with you, did he, Gabriella? What did he do to you? What happened?'

A tear trickled down her face, surprising her because she hadn't known she was going to cry. She lifted her arm and brushed it across her wet eyes like a child.

Stephen moved her arm away and wiped her face gently with a handkerchief. 'I realise it's hard for you to talk about it—that's crystal-clear—but you have to, Gabriella, can't you see that? You've been locking it all away inside you when you should have been talking about it...to someone, if not me. This is the sort of problem that festers if it isn't forced out. You should have seen a psychiatrist long ago; had therapy.'

'That's what Paolo says,' she said, and felt his sharpened attention, the immediate frown.

'So he knows—I suspected he did when you said you trusted him. That was why you came here to him, wasn't it? Because he knew.' Then his voice deepened, angry and harsh. 'Why could you tell him when you apparently can't tell me?'

She gave a quivering sigh. 'I didn't mean to tell him—but we've known each other so long that Paolo sometimes guesses what I'm thinking. I don't know how he does it; I suppose he picks up clues from my face.' Or made leaps of intuition, simply from knowing her so well.

'Maybe I can do that too,' Stephen said roughly. 'It's pretty obvious that something sexually disturbing happened to you. You were attacked, weren't you? Some man attacked you? A stranger? Were you raped?'

'No!' she broke out angrily, struggling away from him and sitting up. 'I told you, no! It wasn't like that.'

'Then what was it? There's something like that—there has to be! Tell me, Gabriella! Talk to me.'

His voice was harsh again, hoarse with angry feeling, and she shrank from it as from fire, afraid of contact with so destructive a force. 'If you can talk to him, you can talk to me!' Stephen muttered and she shuddered.

'When you get like that...that's when you frighten me! You're scaring me now.'

'Like what?' His brows met, his face impatient, baffled. 'Stop talking in riddles! I'm in no mood to play games, Gabriella.'

She looked at him helplessly, knowing that she had to tell him yet afraid to talk about the past. She had to open the locked door, descend into the dark cellar of her past where the ghosts were imprisoned, the memories shut away.

Gabriella didn't know if she had the courage to do it.

CHAPTER SIX

GABRIELLA'S anger came to her rescue again—a deep-burning anger which made her want to hit out at him so much that it gave her a new sort of courage, coursing like adrenalin through her bloodstream. She sat up, swinging her long, slender, silk-clad legs to the floor, her colour coming and going in her delicate face, and knocked Stephen's hand away when he tried to make her lie down again under the fringed canopy of the four-poster bed.

'No! Stop trying to push me around! That's one reason why you frighten me—you crowd in on me too much, won't give me room to breathe; you're always trying to run my life; you don't ask me what I want to do, you just give me orders; you want to make my decisions for me!'

She stood up and walked across the room, as he had done, without even seeing her surroundings, pacing the thickly carpeted floor, her head bent while she thought hard, frowning, her black hair falling forward against her pale cheeks.

Did she want to tell him? Could she bear to talk about it? He was bound to despise her, condemn her—everyone else had at the time. She would never forget the way they had looked at her; that hatred and contempt had marked her for life. She didn't want to see that expression in Stephen's eyes.

Yet would she? She didn't know how he would react. She didn't know him well enough to guess.

She swung to face him again, her blue eyes accusing. 'And another thing... I really don't know you at all, do I? You rushed me into a engagement before I had a chance to get to know you. It never seemed real to me, that engagement. You just said you were in no mood to play games. But what else have you been doing for months? It felt like a game to me; it certainly didn't feel as if I was really engaged, or that we would ever really be married. You've never talked to me about yourself; I don't know what you like, what you want, how you feel—I know very little about you at all.'

He was on his feet too, standing two strides from her, watching her with a black frown.

'You've never shown any interest before. All you had to do was ask questions, but you never asked them.'

It was true; she couldn't deny it. 'But we never talked,' she said. 'I couldn't ask questions when we never talked about anything intimate, never talked about ourselves.'

Quietly he asked, 'So what do you want to know, Gabriella?'

She spread her hands in a furious gesture. 'I don't know... Everything, I suppose. "Talk to me", you said a minute ago. You want me to tell you things I've never told anyone——'

'No one at all?' he broke in harshly.

She shook her head. 'No one at all,' she whispered, her eyes wide and burning.

'Except Paolo!' Stephen bit out and she flinched, hating the snarl of his voice, the threat coming from him.

She had learnt far too young the danger of strong emotions, of a loss of control; she feared it as a burnt child feared fire. She yearned for calm, needed to be safe. She had only ever considered marrying him because he had convinced her that he could give her that stability and security, but she had been fooling herself. She hadn't known him at all, and for that she blamed him, her eyes restlessly touching him and moving away with an angry impatience.

'I explained why I talked to Paolo! You know I did! He is my oldest friend; he's almost family, almost a brother—I know him better than anyone in the world. He was the only one I could risk talking to; there was nobody else!'

'What about your family?'

'There was only my grandmother——' She broke off, biting her lower lip, a small spot of blood showing on it a second later. Her mouth quivering, she added, 'She knew, but—but she couldn't talk about it; she never said a word to me. I certainly couldn't talk to her. We buried it, pretended it hadn't happened.'

'And that's what you've been doing ever since,' he said in a dry tone, and a shiver ran through her. He saw it and said quickly, 'Are you cold?'

She shook her head. 'A ghost walked over my grave.' In more senses than one, she thought; and Stephen frowned as if he had picked up on her thoughts.

'Don't think like that!'

'You mean 'pretend'?' She gave him a melancholy glance. 'I've done so much of that in my life. In fact, that was the worst part of what happened—having to pretend, trying to push it to the back of my mind, trying to make myself forget. Because I couldn't, of course, and neither could my grandmother. It was there, all between us, like a desert we could never cross—a great, empty, burning space where nothing lived or moved.'

'What was?' Stephen asked, but she ignored the question, barely heard it, she was so intent on remembering.

'I knew she hated me, you see,' she whispered. 'Because it was all my fault. I could see it in her eyes. She would be staring at nothing, sitting at the table, at meals, in an armchair in the evening, her face blank, and then she'd suddenly look at me, and I always knew what she had been thinking about. I could feel the bitterness, the resentment, the hatred. It's awful to know you're hated like that. It's very hard to live with, even for a few days, let alone years.'

His frown deepened. 'How old were you then?'

'I lived with her until I was nineteen. She died while I was at college. She had a stroke and couldn't talk or move, and she died a few weeks later. I sat by her bed and held her hand, and tried to talk to her, to tell her how sorry I was, that I knew it was all my fault, that I hadn't wanted any of it to happen. I begged her to forgive me, but she never even looked at me, or showed that she knew I was there. She died without ever looking at me again.'

'She was your father's mother, wasn't she?'

'Yes. My mother's parents died when I was much younger. I was very fond of them, but I never saw them again after my father took me back to England.'

Stephen was watching her intently, his eyes narrowed and silvery. 'You were eleven when you returned to England, weren't you? Did you speak English then? Or had you grown up just speaking Italian?'

There was so much he didn't know about her, so much she didn't know about him; they were practically strangers to each other. This was the first time that they had ever really talked, ever been so frank with each other.

'Italian was my first language,' she explained. 'But my father had always talked to me in English every day so it wasn't difficult for me to go to school when we came over here. I just had to have a few months' coaching in the English language before I went off to boarding-school.'

'Did you like it there?'

She shook her head. 'Not at first. I was lonely, but my father wasn't well enough for me to live with him and he found travelling difficult so I only ever saw him in the holidays.'

'How old were you when your father died?'

'Thirteen,' she said, her eyes haunted. 'I was fourteen that summer, but he died before my birthday. I was still thirteen when he died. It wasn't really a shock; I had been expecting it—we all had—for a long time. He wasn't very strong. He never really recovered from my mother's death; they were very close—her death was a dreadful blow to him. I don't think he wanted to live without her. That was why he brought me back to England—so that his family could take care of me.

'He was always ill; he had to send me to boarding-school, and even in the holidays I saw very little of him. I spent the holidays with...'

She stopped and swallowed, her throat moving visibly. 'With Lara's family. My father lived near them and I visited him on days when he was well enough, but he was too ill to have me living with him. I didn't mind that so much, after a while, because I loved being there. I liked Lara very much, and—and her family... I did miss my father, of course; I kept hoping he would get better and I could live with him all the time, but he got worse, not better, and then the summer when I was coming up to my fourteenth birthday——' She broke off, drawing a long, shaky breath.

'He died,' Stephen said quietly. 'It must have been a bitter blow to you, when you were so young.'

'It was a bad year,' she admitted huskily. 'First my father died, and then... and then my uncle Ben...'

'His brother?'

She swallowed, her slender white throat moving convulsively, and Stephen's gaze sharpened, glittering like needle-points.

'Yes. There were only the two of them. My grandmother only had two children—two sons— and they both died the same summer. She never got over it. I think she began to die too, that summer.' Her mouth quivered. 'I sometimes think my whole life has been punctuated by deaths…my mother's, my father's, my grandmother's…'

There was a silence. She stared at nothing; Stephen stared fixedly at her.

'It was him, wasn't it?' he said at last, and watched her body jerk with reaction, her white face stiffen, her eyes darken.

Tongue-tied, she just stared back at him, but he saw a tell-tale pulse beating in her neck, her hands trembling.

'What…what do you mean? Who?' she whispered.

'You know who I mean. What did he do to you?' He searched her face, his brows together, and said curtly, 'OK, I can see how hard it is for you to talk about it, but it has to come out, Gabriella. You've kept it shut inside you for too long. Why don't I just make a guess? Your uncle tried to——'

'No!' she burst out, shaking so much that she could hardly stand upright. 'Don't. You'll only make it sound…vile…horrible…and it wasn't like that. It wasn't his fault. It was mine. I was the one…'

Her head swam as emotion clouded it; tears welled up in her eyes and fell like rain, running down her cheeks, trickling into her mouth, their salt taste on her tongue. She was shivering from head to foot, her skin icy cold and totally colourless.

Stephen took the two strides between them and picked her up, carried her over to the elaborate four-poster bed and sat down with her on the edge. He pulled up the rose-pink satin quilt which covered it, and wrapped it round her, cocooning her in the thick, soft folds, his arm holding her close to him.

'Cry it out; it's the best thing you could possibly do,' he murmured, rocking her like a child against his heart, and for a few minutes she gave in to her grief, crying helplessly, burrowing into him and feeling the rock-like strength of his body there for her to hide in, feeling his cheek against her hair, his hand stroking her back.

She had had years of practice in hiding her feelings, forcing them down out of sight, pretending they didn't exist. She was an adept at it now. She was afraid of letting go, giving in, afraid that she might go to pieces altogether. She felt herself collapsing inwards like a meringue—crumbling, dissolving.

'No, stop it, let go!' she cried, pushing him away, sitting up, running her hand across her wet eyes. 'I'm fine now,' she insisted.

'Liar,' Stephen said, and caught her face between his two hands, his palms warm against her cold skin. He looked into her startled blue eyes as they lifted to scan his face. 'Stop trying to put off the moment, Gabriella. You are going to tell me what happened to you, what your uncle did, even if I have to lock you up in here and throw away the key until you stop lying to me!'

'He didn't do anything, I keep telling you!' She closed her eyes, fell silent again, then slowly began, her voice barely audible, as if she was talking to herself. 'I was so lonely—I never saw my father and my mother was dead, and school was boring. I lived for the holidays when I went to stay with

Uncle Ben and Aunt Kate; I was fond of them both and I enjoyed having my cousins to play with, being part of a family for a while, feeling I belonged.

'That's the worst part of not having parents or brothers and sisters—you don't belong to anyone. I used to watch my friends being brought to school at the start of term, or being collected at the end of it—they had families, parents who hugged them and looked sad to be saying goodbye to them, or happy to be seeing them again—I envied them so much.

'They used to groan about their parents, complain about them if they had to write letters home each weekend, make jokes about how boring and old-fashioned and fussy they were—and I'd listen and think how I'd give anything to have people who cared enough about me to fuss over me and complain if I didn't write or ring them often enough.'

'Children in happy families always take their lives for granted,' he said drily, grimacing. 'I know I did as a child. Tell me about your uncle and his family—what were your uncle and aunt like?'

He watched her face change, the shutters go up and all expression vanish.

'Never mind,' he quickly said. 'Tell me about Lara—she's older than you, isn't she?'

Relieved to be let off the hook for now, she nodded, relaxing again. 'Yes, she's three years older than me. Her brothers, Sam and Jack, are older than either of us. They're twins; when I first met them, when we first arrived from Italy, they were already in their last year at school—tall, gangling boys, identical. I couldn't tell them apart at all, but

Lara could; she told me to look at their eyebrows. Sam's turned up at the edge like wings; Jack's didn't. That was the only thing about them that wasn't absolutely identical.

'At first I used to have to stare hard to make sure which one it was—but I gradually found I could tell them apart without staring—they had very different personalities, I began to realise. Sam was kind and patient, although he tried to hide it, as if he was ashamed of it. Jack was mischievous; he had a great sense of humour and he loved to tease.'

'They weren't coming to the wedding, were they?'

'No, they both live in Australia. They're married with children. It would have been too far to come just for a wedding and, anyway, I don't know if either of them would have wanted to come even if they lived here. I haven't seen either of them since . . .'

She stopped again, then hurriedly went on. 'They went to college soon after I arrived in England, anyway, so I didn't see much of them after that first year. During the summer holidays they both worked abroad—in France, at hotels, one year, and another year in America, working in summer camps, coaching kids in yachting. That was one of their hobbies; they were both good with boats and very good swimmers. I think they didn't get on with their parents, either. They wanted to get away.'

'But you liked them—your aunt and uncle? You were happy living with them?'

Her face defiant, she said, 'Yes, they were kind, they made me welcome—it must have been a bore for them to be landed with me, but they never let

me see that. Aunt Kate could be irritable sometimes, but she was like that with all of us. Heaven
knows she had enough to cope with; three teenagers are quite a handful, and the house was big
and needed a lot of work. She had help—someone
came in to clean the place—but Aunt Kate did
everything else—all the cooking and shopping.'

'How old was she?'

'In her forties, I suppose. She had been pretty,
but she'd got plump and her hair was grey. She was
a very busy woman, very practical and capable—
she ran things, had her own shop, sat on charity
committees and raised money, had a lot of friends.'

'Did she get on with her husband?'

She knew he had been leading her inexorably to
this question; she dreaded telling him, but she had
no choice any more.

'I think they were both fond of each other. They
didn't quarrel in front of us, but sometimes I think
they argued over money, or Aunt Kate complained
that he wasn't ambitious enough. She wanted a
better lifestyle than he had given her. She had some
very wealthy friends and she wished she could buy
the same sort of clothes, a car as good as any they
had; she was discontented and critical.

'She went out a good deal in the evenings—to
parties, dinner with people. The funny thing was
that she went alone. Uncle Ben wasn't part of her
social life. He wasn't a man who enjoyed going out
much. He was quiet and private; he preferred to
stay at home, read, listen to music. When he had
the time during the summer he liked to go for
country walks—he was very active and could walk

for miles; he could walk us all off our feet—or he'd take a boat out on the river, teach us to row, or play tennis. He gave us all tennis lessons; Lara wasn't very keen, but the boys were and so was I.'

'So in the holidays you saw far more of him than of your aunt, who was always out and busy?'

Their eyes met. Her mouth was dry; she ran her tongue-tip over her lips, nodding.

'Especially at weekends,' she admitted huskily. 'He always thought of things we could all do, but quite often the others argued, didn't want to join in—they were always going off with their friends, leaving me behind.'

She stopped, and then said in a sudden flare of anger, 'He was such a good man! I've never met anyone who was so kind and thoughtful. He spent hours coaching me in tennis, helping me with my holiday projects, talking to me in French, because I was way behind my class in French. I hadn't learnt it in Italy and I had to catch up fast when I went to the boarding-school.

'Uncle Ben spent more time with me than with his own children, but that was their choice, not his. They preferred being with friends their own age.'

'But you didn't?'

She stared at the floor, shuddering, then looked up into his eyes with an angry, desperate honesty.

'I wanted to be with him; I couldn't understand them at all. His wife, his children . . . they treated him in such an offhand way; they laughed at him, ran him down. I adored him. I thought the sun shone out of him. He was a wonderful man. He was so like my father to look at, but he seemed to care about me, and my father no longer cared about anything. I loved Uncle Ben more than anyone in the world.

'Every summer he drove to the school to collect me for the holidays and I'd hang around watching for him through a window, and when I saw his car I'd rush down and hurl myself at him, fling my arms round his neck and cling to him like a limpet while he whirled me round and round with my feet off the ground.

'I was very young for my age, although I didn't realise it then. Oh, in some ways I was independent—living in a boarding-school had taught me to cope with taking care of myself. But in other ways I was quite childish, especially in my emotions; I was always hugging him, kissing him. It never occurred to me that I was no longer a child and it was time I stopped acting as if I were.'

'But your uncle didn't mind all this hugging and kissing?' Stephen asked drily, and her face burned.

She gave him a stricken look, looked away, whispered, 'It never occurred to me to wonder what he felt, what he thought. It should have done—I know that now—but I had no idea about men.'

'How many girls of thirteen would have?' Stephen bit out, and she sighed.

'I was more innocent than most girls of my age. I was a late developer; I was a leggy, skinny girl; I had almost no breasts and I hadn't started having periods. Maybe that's why it was such a shock.

'I think now that I didn't want to grow up—I was clinging on to my childhood because of my mother's death and seeing so little of my father. I hadn't had a chance to follow the usual path kids follow, from being just a child to being a teenager and then an adult. One minute I was a child, the next I had, in effect, no parents and I was on my own.

'I clung to Uncle Ben to save myself from having to face life as a grown-up. It never entered my head that he had different feelings, that he——' She cut off, a sob in her throat, and covered her face with her hands, shaking with tears.

Stephen held her, stroking her hair, murmuring wordlessly. 'Shh... Shh...'

'Don't be kind to me,' she groaned when she could speak without crying. 'It makes it harder; kindness is a trap.'

'Life without kindness is as tasteless as meat without salt,' Stephen said with a crooked little smile, adding, 'Dry your eyes and blow your nose, like a good little girl,' and he produced a clean handkerchief for her to use.

She vaguely resented the gentle mockery. 'I said I was a late developer—I didn't say I hadn't grown up in the end!'

He smiled at her with a charm she couldn't help responding to, a warmth that made her smile back. 'We all have to do that, Gabriella. Life doesn't give us any choice.'

'It certainly didn't give me one! One day I was still just a kid, a bit dreamy, wide-eyed and innocent; the next I was thrown into a maelstrom, and my life was never the same again.'

She gave a little sob, and put her hand over her mouth to stop herself crying again. He took hold of both her hands. 'Tell me the rest, Gabriella. Don't stop now.'

She gave a long sigh, her whole body wrenched by it. 'It was that last summer—the summer my father died. For a few weeks we had very hot weather. One day Uncle Ben and I took a picnic out into the countryside. We walked across some fields into a wood and ate our lunch in the shade.'

She shut her eyes and could see it—midges dancing under the gently moving branches, beyond in the fields the gold of ripening wheat, the dark green of elm and oak with the hot blue sky above them.

'We lay down in the long grass and listened to the birds, and Uncle Ben sat up to watch larks hanging in the sky above the field, so high up you could hear them far better than you could see them; they sounded wonderful.

'I was lying on my back watching him, sleepily, because it was so hot and I had walked a long way and then eaten and I was barely awake. He looked down at me and I smiled at him, feeling terribly happy, and then he changed . . . his face seemed to break up; his voice was sort of hoarse . . . He said he loved me, and that was wonderful, because I needed so badly to be loved. I said I loved him too, of course, and I think I went pink.

'Then suddenly he kissed me . . . not on the cheek the way he usually did, but on the mouth, and in a funny, worrying way, and he didn't stop. He kissed my face and my hair and my neck and my hands and he kept saying how much he loved me;

his voice sounded so weird. He was very flushed and he was shaking.

'I began to get frightened after a while, but I didn't know what to do. I just lay there—and then he...he began...touching me. I wasn't so innocent that I didn't know what he wanted to do, and I was horrified. I felt sick; I went into panic; I began screaming and fighting him off; I scratched his face and kicked...and then—and then...'

She was hyperventilating, breathing so fast that she could hardly get the words out; she wanted to finish telling him quickly; she wanted to get it over with now that she had started. She had shut it all inside her head for so long—it was a terrible relief to say it out loud, and the words just poured out of her.

'There were some people across the other side of the field—ramblers, on a walk, like us. We hadn't even noticed them coming towards us but when I began to scream they came running; they pulled him off and one of the men hit him, knocked him out. He just went limp and lay there, and that frightened me even more—I thought they had killed him; he looked as if he was dead. I felt the most terrible guilt.'

Stephen's face was grim. 'You had no reason to feel guilty!'

'Didn't I?' she asked, her eyes wild. 'Don't you see...? It would never have happened if I hadn't acted the way I did. He was lonely and unhappy and he misunderstood how I felt about him.'

'You were a child, he was your uncle. You were in his care—if there was guilt, it was his. Gabriella, try to step outside it all. How would you feel if you read a story in a newspaper about a girl of thirteen and her middle-aged uncle? Who would you think was to blame? The child or the man?'

'You'd have to know what really happened!'

He sighed, his expression hardening. 'Well, never mind. Tell me what happened next.'

She shut her eyes. 'I don't know. It was so confusing; everyone was shouting and asking questions and I was so scared. One of the ramblers went off and called the police. It never occurred to me that they might do that.

'The first thing I knew was when a police car arrived and then an ambulance. I was taken to the hospital where I saw a doctor. The two hours I spent there were——' she groaned, shuddering '—horrible. I was so embarrassed and scared. I kept telling them nothing had happened, but they didn't believe me. They made me take all my clothes off; they took them away for examination; they examined me. I was petrified.

'Eventually the police arrived and took me to the police station where I had to answer a lot more questions. My uncle was there but I didn't see him. After I'd made a statement I was sent to my grandmother's. She was so angry with me that she couldn't even speak to me at first, then she made me tell her exactly what had happened, and she called me some terrible names, said it was all my fault, and that she and Aunt Kate had seen me always hanging around him, wanting him to notice me. I'd brought it on myself; I was the one to blame, she said.'

Stephen inhaled sharply. 'Ah, so that's why you blame yourself! She put the idea into your head.'

'It was already there! I loved Uncle Ben, I was appalled at what was going on, I desperately wanted to stop it happening but there was nothing I could do—it had all gone too far. My grandmother said she couldn't bear to see me; she sent me back to school a week later. It was like being in a nightmare. I had to pretend nothing was wrong; I couldn't talk about it to anyone.

'I didn't know my uncle had been charged—I don't know what with exactly; I think they called it a sexual assault. They hadn't named me, of course—I was a minor—but I discovered later that it was the talk of the neighbourhood. Everyone knew some version of the scandal; and what they didn't know they embroidered.

'People stood outside his house and stared, and Aunt Kate sent her children away to stay with her family in Scotland. My uncle was released on bail. God knows what Aunt Kate said to him, but he killed himself, two weeks later, with sleeping pills. Aunt Kate sold the house and went back to Scotland. I never saw her again, but my grandmother let me go back to stay with her in the holidays.

'She told me Uncle Ben had written her a suicide note, asking her to be kind to me, saying it was all his fault. She said she knew that wasn't true—it was my fault—but it was the last thing he asked her to do, so she was having me back, but I needn't think she had forgotten what I'd done.'

She stopped speaking abruptly, out of breath, trembling, and Stephen watched her, his eyes sombre. 'Are you telling me that your grandmother went on blaming you for the rest of her life? How could she, when you were just a child and——?'

'He was her son,' said Gabriella. 'They both died that summer, both her sons—it broke her heart. I broke her heart.'

Roughly, Stephen contradicted her. 'He broke her heart—first by trying to abuse a child he was supposed to be protecting, and then by being so weak and cowardly that he couldn't face the consequences of what he had done.' His voice was harsh, scornful. 'You aren't guilty of anything but a normal, childish need to love and be loved. He knew you were still just a child—his brother's child. You were the last person he should have hurt like that.'

She shook her head. 'With one part of my mind I know you're right, but you didn't know him. He was a very kind man, a good man, and he did love me. I think, looking back, that he was going through some sort of mid-life crisis; I don't think his marriage had given him what he needed, and he grabbed at my love for him, misunderstood the way I felt.'

'And left you scarred for life, unable to let yourself have feelings in case you lose control the way he did that summer day in the woods. That's what he did to you, isn't it, Gabriella? Left you terrified of passion, of any intense emotion.'

She sat silent, pale and exhausted. She was too tired to argue any more; she was too tired even to cry any more. She felt as though she had been through a new ordeal more terrible than anything else that had happened to her; her body was limp with weariness. She wanted to fall on to a bed and sleep for days, drown in sleep, escape into oblivion.

'Will you take me back to my hotel, please?' she pleaded, her eyes dark-ringed. 'I can't talk any more tonight, I'm so tired. Please let me go back to my hotel. I need to be alone for a while.'

Stephen frowned at her, hesitated, then said flatly, 'Will you give me your word of honour that you won't run away again?'

She nodded. 'Yes, word of honour...' She would have said anything he wanted her to, if only to get away from him. 'Anyway, I couldn't run any-where—I'm dead on my feet.'

She got up, staggering slightly as she began to walk, and Stephen quickly moved to put an arm round her shoulders. She was grateful for the warmth of his body, for his strength. She wanted to lean on him, but she couldn't let herself give in to the temptation—he might misunderstand.

She had promised that she wouldn't run away again, but that didn't mean she had changed her mind about marrying him. If Stephen thought he could talk her into going back with him and going through with the wedding after all he was deluding himself. Nothing would persuade her to marry him now.

CHAPTER SEVEN

STEPHEN dropped her at the entrance to her hotel. Gabriella had sat in silence all the way along the narrow, winding roads, her body limp and her mind empty. She didn't even notice that the dripping, damp mist had cleared and the night sky was deep blue, clear and full of stars. She didn't hear the murmur of the lake just below them or realise that there was no other traffic around, and that the little villages and towns were silent and dark. She wasn't thinking of anything, or feeling anything. She was far too tired.

When the car stopped she stirred and looked out of the window, realised they had arrived, and saw then the mist had gone, but without surprise or even interest.

Stephen came round to open the door. He took her elbow to help her out. She pulled away from him gently, without looking at him or saying anything. She did not want him to touch her.

She moved slowly because she knew that if she moved fast she might fall down. She was barely in control of her body. She had to concentrate on every movement like a baby learning to walk, her head bent, her face averted from him.

'I'll see you safely inside,' Stephen said, walking beside her. She felt his intent gaze on her; it was like the touch of his hand, too disturbing to be borne. She didn't have the energy to cope with him, not now. 'And I'll be back tomorrow morning, at about ten-thirty,' he added when she didn't answer. 'Sleep late; have your breakfast in bed. You'll feel better after a good night's rest.'

He was giving her orders again, trying to run her life. She stirred herself, forced at last to reply. 'I'm not coming back with you, Stephen,' she told him wearily. 'I'm staying here for a while.'

'We'll talk about that tomorrow.' His voice was cool, but carried that unselfconscious arrogance which annoyed her. He was so sure of himself, so convinced that he must have his own way.

'No, we won't! I've decided to stay and I'm not going to be talked out of it!' There was a last flicker of energy in her raised voice, in the impatient little flush which invaded her cheeks. She had had enough for the moment. The last thing she needed was another confrontation, but at the same time she did not want him dictating to her. She knew what she wanted to do and she was not going to allow Stephen to bully her.

He shot a probing glance at her, read the anger and obstinacy in her face, shrugged, then opened one of the big glass doors which bore the gilded crest of the hotel on them.

'Goodnight, Gabriella,' he said, with the same cool arrogance.

'Goodnight,' she said, walking past him into the echoing marble-floored vestibule of the hotel. For a second she thought he might come with her, but the door swung shut and he vanished back into the dark blue of the Italian night.

She collected her key from the night porter, a man she had not seen before, thin and neat in his uniform jacket, in his forties, with a moustache and slicked-back black hair.

When she said her name and room number he gave her a very odd look, his eyes sharpening.

'Ah, yes. There is a gentleman waiting to see you, *signorina*. He has been waiting for three hours.'

Gabriella did a double-take, blue eyes widening, the pale skin around them stretching into a mask. 'A gentleman?' Then she realised who it must be and added breathlessly, 'Where is he?'

'In the main lounge, *signorina*.' The porter gave a little cough, veiled disapproval in his face. 'At this hour, please do not raise your voices; you might disturb other guests.'

Gabriella flushed, looked up at the old mahogany-cased clock ticking on the wall behind the porter, and was amazed to see that it was past midnight. She and Stephen had been together for nearly four hours!

Without another word, she turned away and walked through into the long lounge which led to the garden terrace. As her footsteps echoed on the marble floor there was a movement in one of the chairs and then Paolo got up, dropping the magazine he had been reading.

'At last! Are you OK?' His face was drawn, anxiety in his eyes. He came towards her fast, looked down searchingly into her face.

She managed a pale smile, nodding.

He groaned. 'I've been out of my mind. I wanted to ring the police but I didn't know what to say to them—it wasn't easy to explain why I was worried. So I've been sitting here for what seems an eternity, waiting for you. The night porter has tried to throw me out a couple of times, but I wouldn't go until I'd seen you.'

'You shouldn't have waited! You must be very tired, Paolo. You look as if you are. Didn't you get Stephen's message saying I was with him?'

'Of course I did; why do you think I was so worried?' Paolo took both her hands, then noticed the bandaging on her palm, stiffened and stared down at it, frowning. 'Gabi, what's this? What happened? He wasn't violent?'

She sighed, shook her head. 'No, of course not! I had an accident; I was clumsy—knocked over a glass lamp and then stupidly tried to pick up the pieces in a hurry and cut myself.'

'He scared you into it, then,' Paolo rightly concluded and she gave him a wry look. He knew her far too well.

'Maybe, but... I'm sorry, I'm really too tired to talk tonight—I'll tell you all about it next time I see you.'

'Tomorrow morning?'

She hesitated. 'He's coming at ten-thirty.'

Paolo's face tightened. 'Then I'll be here at ten.'

She shook her head. 'I will have to see him alone, for the last time, to make him understand that I'm not going back to London, I'm staying here, and... and that it's over... between us.'

Paolo's brows jerked together. 'Haven't you told him yet? About your uncle? Gabriella, you must...'

'I have,' she said shortly.

He watched her with fixed attention. 'You told him everything?'

Their eyes met. She nodded, her face sad and weary. 'Everything; I told him everything.'

'How did he react?' Paolo's gaze hunted over her face. 'From the look of you he wasn't sympathetic—if he hurt you, I'll kill him!'

She managed a quivering smile. 'Don't be so bloodthirsty!' Then she remembered Stephen's face while he'd listened to her and gave a grimace of surprise. 'Actually, he was very sympathetic. But I can't talk now; I'm so tired, Paolo—I feel as if I've been through a wringer, emotionally. I really must go to bed. Ring me tomorrow afternoon.' She leaned forward and kissed his cheek, finding his skin cool against her lips. He had been sitting here in the hotel for hours; anxiety had made him pale and cold. 'You must be tired too. Go home to bed, Paolo,' she said, smiling at him. 'And thank you for worrying, and for being here for me.'

'You're my oldest friend, Gabi. I'll always be here for you,' Paolo said, kissing her back lightly on the cheek, and she was very touched by the gesture, by the words.

Her spirits lifted. She walked to the lift, hearing Paolo leave, his footsteps ringing on the marble floor, the swish of the hotel's glass doors opening and closing, before the night quiet descended. Apart from the porter behind his desk, the whole hotel was asleep.

Back in her room overlooking the dark lake, she undressed automatically, folding her clothes in a pile on a chair, and went into the bathroom. A few

minutes later she slid down into bed, reached across
to the bedside lamp and turned it off. The darkness
was a deep relief. A long sigh wrenched her. She
lay listening to the distant sound of the lake lapping
at its shores, the murmur of a little wind across the
water. Her eyes closed, and she fell into a deep,
dreamless sleep—the sleep of exhaustion, of utter
blankness.

When she woke up, sunlight dappled the walls.
She felt light and cool; all the weariness had gone,
and taken with it the strain she had felt for days.
Staring out of the window, through the gauze curtains, she saw a blue sky and, beneath it, the snow-
capped outlines of the mountains on the far side
of the lake. It was a beautiful morning. She felt no
urge to move, or do anything; she just lay there
contentedly staring at that miraculous view.

Yawning, she reluctantly looked round at her
bedside clock, realising that she could not lie there
all day, and was amazed to see that it was nearly
ten. Stephen would be here in half an hour!

If she wasn't downstairs he would come up here
to find her—he mustn't find her in bed!

Hurriedly, she got up and went to the bathroom,
used the lavatory, showered, quickly blow-dried her
wet hair, slid into a towelling robe, then rang
downstairs and ordered breakfast from Room
Service, having realised that they would have
stopped serving in the dining-room.

She fell easily into Italian, asking if they could
bring her some breakfast.

'*Posso avere la prima colazione in
camera, signore?*'

She hoped that they had not stopped serving breakfast altogether.

But the man who had answered the phone agreed amiably. '*Sì, signorina*, we will bring it to your room at once. What would you like?'

She ordered a simple continental meal—orange juice, coffee, croissants. She was quite hungry, she realised suddenly, surprising herself.

While she waited for the food to arrive she put on crisp white cotton underwear, white jeans and a navy blue and white striped T-shirt, slid her feet into white moccasins, then smoothed a little foundation cream into her face, brushed her mouth with lipstick and was just clipping earrings into her ears when the room-service waiter knocked briskly on the door.

It was the same boy who had told her about the geography of the lake. He beamed at her delightedly.

'*Buongiorno, signorina! Come sta?*'

'*Benissimo, grazie*,' she said, smiling back at him and still feeling light as air and free as a bird. It must have been the relief of having told Stephen the truth, of no longer having to worry about what to say to him. She hadn't realised until now just how much of a strain it had been, never talking about the past, trying to suppress it from her mind, trying to forget it had ever happened. Paolo was right; she had let the past destroy the present. The poison of her memories had darkened her entire life.

'You would like me to take the tray out on to the balcony?' asked the waiter and she nodded, opening the windows wide to let him walk outside.

He lingered for a moment or two, setting out the woven basket of toast and croissants, a white damask napkin covering them to keep them hot, little pots of marmalade, honey and jam, a white bone-china butter dish, a large silver coffee-pot, the matching cream jug and sugar bowl, the cup and saucer, before he poured her first cup for her. While he deftly worked he talked to her about a cabaret they were going to have that night at the hotel next door.

'A pop group, and dancers. My friend who works there says the girls just wear a few sequins and a couple of feathers! And he says they can kick their legs above their heads! And turn cartwheels. They're almost boneless, like rubber. He's going to smuggle me in to see the show from the back of the room. Oh, they're a go-ahead bunch, next door, not like this place. The manager here shudders at the very idea of loud music, and as for dancers like that...' The boy pulled a droll face, waving his hands contemptuously. 'He would have a heart attack if you suggested it to him!'

'Did you?' Gabriella sat down at the table and picked up her orange juice, sipping it with pleasure; it was freshly squeezed, thickened with tiny fragments of orange, but cold from a fridge and very refreshing.

The young waiter was laughing. 'Me? Suggest he had a cabaret here? He'd fire me on the spot.'

Behind them someone pushed open the door of the room, which the waiter had left ajar when he arrived. Giving a hurried look over his shoulder, the young waiter stopped laughing.

'*Scusi, Signorina,*' he said quickly and turned to go.

Gabriella looked after him and saw Stephen framed in the doorway. Her heart almost stopped; she felt a sharp kick of pain in her chest and her breath caught.

He came out on to the balcony, stepping out of the path of the departing waiter, his face impassive. The boy muttered a polite greeting, Stephen nodded to him and answered in English.

'Good morning. Could you bring another cup and some more coffee?'

'*Sì, signore,*' the waiter said, his eyes curious. He had seen her with Paolo; he must be wondering which of the two men she was actually involved with—or perhaps he thought she had both men on a string? The idea made Gabriella flush. What sort of reputation was she getting at the hotel? The thought hadn't occurred to her before, but she didn't like the obvious answer.

When the boy had gone Stephen stood beside the table, his grey eyes narrowly searching her face for clues about her mood and state of mind. He was far too clever and he saw too much; she resented that probing stare, the mind behind it trying to probe her own mind.

'You look much better this morning,' he drawled, his lean body at ease as he leaned over the back of one of the chairs. 'How do you feel?'

'Fine,' she said warily, not wanting to tell him too much.

His mouth twisted ironically, as if he did not believe her. 'Did you sleep?'

'Very well.' There was defiance in the lift of her head. She had been betrayed into saying too much yesterday—she wasn't going to do that again.

His grey eyes bored into hers, his face sardonic. 'Good. I wish I had. I got an hour or so, no more than that.'

'Sorry,' she said helplessly, not sure what to make of that answer, whether he was blaming her, accusing her, or simply telling the truth.

She tried not to stare, fighting to seem calm and indifferent, but she was neither. The moment he had walked out on to the balcony she had felt her whole body come alive. She had felt as if the sun had just come out on a grey day, flooding her with light and warmth. That the mere sight of him could have such incredible impact on her—wasn't that scary?

He was wearing casual clothes—lightweight pale grey trousers, a white sweater so fine and delicate that it was like a spider's web, and under that a black shirt worn open at the neck and without a tie. She had rarely seen him dressed so casually. It looked good on him, but then whatever he wore looked terrific. In his usual dark city suits and immaculate white shirts and silk ties he was deeply sexy; in formal evening-suits he took your breath away.

Hungrily, she absorbed every detail of the way he looked this morning—his dark hair brushed flat and smooth, his face clean-shaven. He looked cool and elegant—you would never have guessed that he hadn't slept, but then Gabriella had never been able to read what was going on inside Stephen. He had always been a mystery to her. Nothing had changed in that respect, had it? After yesterday he knew far more about her, but what did she know about him?

He had all his usual poised alertness, those grey eyes watchfully intelligent, hunting over her own face and picking up what was happening inside her. It disturbed her that he should be able to read her feelings while she never seemed able to get inside his head in the same way. She felt her pulse-rate pick up, felt her body vibrate with awareness of him and was shaken and taken aback by the intensity of her instant physical response to him.

It wasn't fair! she thought, filled with childish resentment. Why couldn't she control those feelings? She tried, God knew. She didn't want to feel that way; she would have given anything to be able to look at him without this terrifying, dizzying reaction, without her breathing quickening, her blood whizzing through her veins, her skin perspiring as if she had suddenly found herself under a burning sun.

Why couldn't she fight it? She had to; somehow she had to—if she didn't, how could she tell him to go and make him believe that she meant it? She was giving herself away too painfully with every second of the time they were together, every look she gave him, every tiny betraying response.

She tore her gaze away and looked down at the

table, at the coffee-pot, the covered basket of croissants and toast, the half-drunk glass of orange juice.

'I was just going to eat my breakfast.'

'Eat it, then,' Stephen said coolly, and sat down on the other chair beside the table, his gaze flicking over the food. 'It looks very good.'

She moistened her dry lips. 'Have you eaten? Have one of these croissants; I only want one and there are several in the basket.'

'No, thank you; I'm not hungry.'

'Neither am I.' She had been until he arrived. Now her appetite had gone.

He leaned over and picked up the glass of juice, held it to her mouth. 'You need the sugar.'

He was far too close. Their eyes met and her heart did a sideways skip. She took the glass away from him and gulped some juice, her eyes lowered, put the glass down on the table, knowing that she was trembling, then forced herself to start eating a croissant, before drinking some of the coffee the waiter had poured for her.

'Lovely view,' Stephen drawled a few moments later, and she risked a glance at him, saw him staring out across the lake, sunlight glittering on his smooth skin and the jet-black hair. Her bones seemed to turn to water. She had to put down her cup because her hand was shaking and she was afraid she might drop the coffee.

Stephen turned back towards her, and her pulses leapt again. His grey eyes gleamed suddenly with soft mockery as he observed the agitation in her face, her shaking fingers.

'What's the matter, Gabriella?' he murmured, and she felt her skin run with hot colour.

She tried to lie her way out of it. 'Nothing! I...burnt my fingers on the coffee-pot. I...you... Oh, you make me nervous! That's all.' The dry amusement in his eyes made her anger flare up again, and she snapped at him, 'Why won't you go? I meant what I said to you last night—I'm not coming back to England yet. In fact, I might stay here. I may get a job, work in a local hotel. Please leave me alone, Stephen. Go back to London.'

He didn't look amused now; his brows had jerked together in a frown. 'I'll go back to London when I'm ready,' he bit out, and she shrugged crossly at him.

'Well, that's your affair, but stay away from me from now on! I don't want to see you any more. It's over.'

'Is it?' He got to his feet, and at once she was swamped with alarm.

She got up too, tried to back. 'Don't you...' She found herself right up against the balcony rail and stumbled, almost falling over it with a startled cry.

'Are you trying to kill yourself?' Stephen muttered harshly, grabbing at her.

Off balance, having frightened herself by almost falling, she couldn't think clearly enough to stop him. His arm was round her waist, his hand right under her breast, so that she felt his fingers touching her with an intimacy that made her head spin.

She caught her breath audibly and her eyes closed. The next second he lifted her right off her feet, up into the air, and she clutched at him, dizzy and breathless.

'No, put me down . . . Don't . . .'

'And let you fall off this damned balcony? Not on your life.' He carried her off the balcony into her bedroom, ignoring her struggles. 'Keep still; you're making me angry,' he muttered with his face down against her hair, the sound of his voice muffled.

Held high, against his heart, Gabriella heard the deep, ragged beat of it under her ear.

He sat down on the bed, still holding her, so that she lay across his lap like a child, except that she did not feel in the least childlike—her emotions were far too troubled and adult.

'Let go of me,' she whispered, wishing her body would not pulse with such hot awareness of him.

'Why did you ever say you'd marry me?' he asked, taking her by surprise so that her blue eyes widened and without pausing to think she blurted out the truth.

'I don't know.'

His brows met. 'Oh, come on, Gabriella!' he bit out impatiently. 'Of course you know—you're not stupid!'

'No, I'm not,' she threw back, very flushed. 'But that night is just a blur—I can't remember much about it. It all happened too fast. We were having dinner as usual one minute, and the next——' She broke off, her eyes confused with the memories of how she had felt. 'I wasn't expecting you to propose. I hadn't thought ahead, about where it was leading—seeing you, I mean, dating you . . .'

His mouth was hard, angry; his grey eyes flashed. 'What the hell did you think I wanted? I hadn't tried to get you into bed, but I kept asking you out. You must have realised I wanted more than friendship. I'm not a teenager, I'm a man, Gabriella—a perfectly normal male with all the usual needs and desires.'

She was so tense that she was shaking. She had to swallow twice before she could stammer, 'I know—I . . . Oh, I can't explain . . . I was just sleepwalking . . .'

'Sleepwalking?' he snarled. 'What in God's name does that mean? What are you talking about?'

Tears prickled behind her lids. 'Don't keep shouting at me! How can I think straight when you keep shouting?' She tried to struggle up, get to her feet. 'And will you let me go?'

His arm tightened round her; she couldn't get free. Stephen looked down into her eyes, his face taut and darkly flushed.

'Stop fighting me, Gabriella,' he said through his teeth. 'I'm sorry if I shouted—I'll try to stay calm— but don't fight me or I won't be responsible for what happens. Now, what exactly did you mean when you said you were sleepwalking?'

She shut her eyes and lay still in the circle of his arms. The trouble was that it was so tempting to feel the warmth and security of his body against her, to be held and protected. She yearned to yield to it, but she was still so afraid—loving was far too dangerous. You could get hurt, or you could hurt someone. Love was a road that could lead you right off the edge of a precipice.

'Come on, Gabriella,' he coaxed. 'Tell me what you meant. How can I understand if you won't explain?'

'It's hard to put it into words,' she whispered. 'Of course I was wide awake—but sleepwalking is the nearest I can get to what it's like, because sleepwalkers don't see where they're going, or realise when they're in danger. They fall out of windows or down the stairs, because they aren't looking— they're walking with their eyes shut, in a daze. That's how it is with me; this isn't the first time I've sleepwalked into disaster. That's why it happened with . . . with him . . .'

She stopped, swallowing, and felt his hand move on her hair, stroking it slowly, softly, soothing her.

The gentleness undermined her even more. She wanted to cry. Her body went limp against him, leaned on him, taking in the warmth of his body through his clothes, comforted by it as well as by the caressing movement of his hand on her head.

Did he care about her? She hadn't thought he did, perhaps because she had been afraid to hope that he might; she was still afraid. It was so long since anyone had loved her. She needed love with an ache that was intolerable, yet she was afraid of what she needed because the only time that she had let herself care about anyone and known that she was loved in turn it had all ended in a horror that she could not bear to remember even now.

'Your uncle?' His voice was so low and soft.

'Yes,' she huskily admitted. 'I sleepwalked into that. I should have realised he ... that ... But I didn't, because I never stopped to think—I just felt so happy, knowing he was really fond of me. I didn't understand what was really going on. I was blind—and the same thing happened with you.

'I should never have gone out with you, or let things go so far, but I was in a sort of trance. I didn't have any control, any idea where I was going—I just let things drift, day after day, and when you asked me to marry you I was taken aback—I hadn't expected it—and I didn't know what to say, but I——' She broke off, swallowing, then said in a rush, 'I thought we might be happy; I hoped ... I thought it would work out, until——' She broke off again, shuddering, and felt his body stiffen against her.

'Until?' he prompted tersely and she sighed.

'The party ...'

'At last we're getting to the truth! You ran away because I scared you that night. That's the truth, isn't it? I lost control, and you suddenly realised that once we were married I'd expect rather more from you than a polite kiss or two.'

Her face burned. A pulse beat in her neck, another in her temples; panic ran through her and made her throat close up.

Stephen took hold of her chin and turned her face up towards him; she had to meet his gaze, her blue eyes wide with terror.

'Hadn't it occurred to you to wonder what I wanted from you, Gabriella? Why on earth did you think I asked you to marry me?' His eyes darkened, heat suddenly burning in them, and she trembled even more. 'Do I have to tell you?' The hand beneath her breast moved, slid under her navy blue and white striped top, and she drew a fierce breath as she felt the warmth of his fingers slide inside her bra to caress her naked breast.

'No, please! Don't!'

Stephen lowered his head as she cried out; a second later his mouth softly touched her eyelids, kissed them shut.

'I knew you were shy; I knew you were nervous,' he whispered. 'Why else do you think I was so careful never to panic you or go too fast? I was taking it slowly, taking my time, and it wasn't easy for me.'

Gabriella was lost in darkness, her lids fluttering but not lifting because she didn't want to see that look on his face again. It scared her too much. The desire in his eyes sent shivers down her back.

'Stop trembling,' he whispered, his mouth silkily moving over her face, brushing kisses like the flicker of a butterfly's wings on her lashes, on her cheeks, along her nose.

'Let me show you how it can be between a man and woman, when there's no guilt or fear. Gabriella . . . you don't need to be afraid . . .'

He carefully removed the earrings from her ears. She heard them drop on to the bedside table with a little chink.

'I. . .I can't. . .' she groaned as his mouth pressed against the lobe of one ear; then she felt his tongue slide inside, follow the curled softness of the interior, making her shiver with pleasure at the soft, warm invasion.

'I'm not frightening you now, am I?' he murmured into her ear, and his hand moved again against her breast. The warmth of his palm cupped the naked flesh, his thumb softly caressed the hard, aroused nipple. 'This isn't frightening, is it?'

A sensual shudder ran through her. No, he wasn't frightening her; this was not fear that she was experiencing. It was an almost agonising arousal, a sensuality so piercing that it hurt, but then desire was pain, as she had learnt a long time ago.

Pain and fear, guilt and anguish were the consequences of desire, and Gabriella was terrified of being dragged down into that inevitable spiral again. Torn between what she needed and wanted and what she feared, she groaned, opening her eyes, as white now as she had been red a few moments ago.

'No, please don't, Stephen. I can't bear it.'

He wasn't listening. His head was moving down her body, slowly, so slowly, until his mouth reached her throat and his lips parted, his teeth softly grazing her skin.

'Stephen . . . no, don't!'

His mouth moved on again and her whole body arched in a paroxysm of desire which pierced her like a knife as she felt his lips on her breast, opening around her nipple, sucking it into his warm, moist mouth.

The intimacy shocked her, excited her—she cried out silently, her own mouth open in a soundless, ecstatic, tortured cry of pleasure beyond anything she had ever felt in her life before.

'Give in to it, darling,' he muttered, his tongue hot on her cool flesh. 'Stop fighting me. Once you stop fighting you'll realise it was fear itself you were frightened of, not me or passion. You're still hooked into the past, still tied up with guilt over what happened to you when you were just a child. It wasn't your fault. You don't need to feel guilty or afraid. Break free; make love to me; touch me.'

He grabbed one of her hands and lifted it, pushed it under his sweater and inside his shirt, and held it palm down against his naked chest. She felt his heart beating under her fingers, the blood running through his veins, his life under her hand.

Of their own accord her fingers seemed to press deeper into him, their tips caressing his warm skin, the rough dark hairs prickling against her. She followed the downward track of the hair, and felt his breathing quicken.

Stephen suddenly sank backwards, taking her with him. Startled, she found herself on her back on the bed, with him lying above her, his knee nudging her legs apart, his muscled thigh pushing in between them.

'No...' she gasped.

He muttered thickly, 'Gabriella...you want me; tell me you want me. You do, don't you? God, I want you, you know that, Gabriella; I must have you. Now, Gabriella, now.'

His voice was hoarse, barely audible, and she stiffened, her eyes opening again, wide and dark blue with shock.

There was something so strange in his voice—a roughness, like triumph, a harshness like rage. It was not, surely not, the voice of a man in love? Or a man who cared for the woman he was talking about making love to?

Had he come after her just to find out why she had run away, why she had jilted him on their wedding-day and left him practically standing at the altar? Oh, no doubt he had wanted to know what was behind her flight—he had been determined to find out why she had run away—but what if his motive in coming after her had not been simply to get her to confide in him? What if he had wanted more than the answer to the question why?

Had Stephen pursued her to get his revenge? Sick panic clenched her stomach.

It wouldn't be so surprising, would it? She had humiliated him publicly, made him a laughing-stock. A jilted bridegroom was always a comic figure, and Stephen Durrant was not a man to shrug off the experience of being made to look a fool. He would want to get his own back on anyone who had done that.

What if this had been his game-plan all along, from the minute he had caught up with her? It was so simple, wasn't it? He would seduce her, take her to bed and then walk away afterwards and forget all about her.

She shuddered, and he muttered, 'Gabriella, Gabriella, relax ... give in to it ...'

Give in? she thought wildly. Give in to what? If she was right, and Stephen was cold-bloodedly bent on getting her into bed in revenge, it had nothing to do with love or desire—no such hot emotions were driving him at this moment.

If she did give in—if she gave herself to him, let the sensuality of his mouth and hands seduce her— he would take her body with hatred, a cold conquest in which the only pleasure would be in the pain he meant to inflict on her afterwards.

Revenge was a satisfying of cold rage, a tortured way of dealing with your own pain by inflicting it on others. He would use her, and afterwards ...

She shivered in shame and fear at the thought of how he would tell her what he had just done to her, precisely what he really felt about her. If he had followed her here relentlessly to get his revenge it would be all the sweeter for having humiliated her in private, as she had humiliated him in public.

If that happened to her she would want to die.

She felt his hands dragging off her jeans and began to fight him, almost crazy suddenly, not caring whether or not she hurt him, kicking and scratching like a wild cat.

'Gabrella ... what the ...? Stop it,' he grunted, trying to calm her, trying to hold her down on the bed by her shoulders, his body imposing its weight on her; but that only made her more determined than ever to get away, to escape the powerful body she found so piercingly attractive and yet feared so much.

She was sobbing and yelling at him now, almost demented. 'Let me go... I don't want you to touch me... I won't let you do this to me...'

He sounded shaken, his voice deep and startled. 'Stop it, Gabriella! What's the matter with you? Why have you gone crazy like this? I'm not going to hurt you—that's the last thing I'd do... Calm down...'

'Not until you let me go!'

At that instant somebody knocked on her door with a sharp, peremptory tattoo. Stephen froze, lifting his head to listen. 'What the hell...? Who on earth can that be?'

Gabriella took advantage of his distraction to dislodge him. She bucked like a wild horse, her body writhing furiously in the effort to push him away.

With a grunt of surprise, Stephen fell backwards, but he was still holding on to her, and he dragged her with him so that they both fell on the floor with a loud thud.

Gabriella was winded for a few seconds, her heart crashing into her ribs and her breathing deafening her. Stephen was breathing fast too, his body tangled with hers, their arms and legs meshed together.

While she was trying to pull herself together, the knocking on the door came again—but louder, more peremptory, and at the same time the man outside spoke loudly, close to the door.

'Gabriella?' The voice made her start, her blue eyes opening wide. 'Gabriella, are you OK? It's Paolo. What's going on? What was that noise? Open the door.'

CHAPTER EIGHT

'WHAT'S he doing here?' Stephen glared down at her and in his eyes Gabriella read jealousy and suspicion. 'Were you expecting him? Had you arranged for him to come?'

Could he be jealous if he didn't care about her? Her mind swam with confusion again, and the usual uncertainty and insecurity. If only she knew what really went on inside him; if only she understood him. But she had never yet understood the way a man's mind worked. They were a mystery to her. Did other women understand them? she wondered. Were they so different from women? Was it quite impossible to guess what made them tick? Or was it just her? Was she too stupid to work out what happened inside their heads?

Paolo banged on the door even louder, his voice rising. 'Gabriella, let me in. What's wrong? Is he in there? Won't he let you open the door? Shall I go and get the manager to use a pass key?'

Stephen swore through his teeth. 'Damn him, he would, wouldn't he?'

'Yes,' she whispered, because Paolo was the one man she had ever vaguely understood and she knew that he would do what he had threatened. Uneasily she watched Stephen get to his feet, raking back his tousled black hair, tucking his shirt back into his trousers with an impatient gesture.

'I'll get the manager, then, shall I?' Paolo repeated.

'Wait a moment, Paolo,' Gabriella called unsteadily, fumbling with shaking fingers to tidy herself as she hurried to let him in.

'I'll do it,' Stephen muttered, but she shook her head without looking at him.

'No, I will; this is my room.' She pushed past him, zipping up her jeans, pulling down her T-shirt, smoothing her hair as she stumbled across the room to the door, to unlock it and begin to open it.

As she did so, Paolo almost crashed through it, using his shoulder to widen the gap. Behind him, in the corridor, she saw the stares and fascinated, shocked faces of other guests who had come out of their rooms on hearing all the noise and were waiting to see the outcome.

They gaped at her, taking in her dishevelled state with widening eyes. Turning crimson, Gabriella hurriedly backed out of sight again. She shut the door and looked round at Paolo, who had halted in the centre of the room, confronting Stephen, his body language as clear as a bell—shoulders set belligerently, feet apart as if poised to spring at the other man, his hands screwed into fists.

'What have you been doing to her, you bastard?' he snarled in angry, rapid Italian.

'Who the hell do you think you are, talking to me like that?' Stephen threw back, using the same language, and bristling like a dog about to bite. 'Gabriella is marrying me, not you, and whatever happens between me and her is no business of yours, so just you stay out of it.'

'I'll do nothing of the kind! I'm the closest thing to family she's got and I'm not going to stand by and let you hurt her, so get out of here and leave her alone!'

'Hurt her? What do you think I am? Gabriella, tell him I wasn't hurting you!' Stephen's grey eyes flashed to her face, the glitter in them demanding, insisting that she back him up.

She couldn't make a sound—she was too disturbed. Stephen's features tightened into a grim mask, as if she had hit him across the face.

'Gabriella! Tell him the truth!'

'Yes, tell me the truth, Gabriella,' Paolo said with angry emphasis. 'Don't tell me whatever lies he wants you to give me. I'm here now; you don't need to be frightened of him. Was he hurting you?'

She shook her head. 'No, of course not.'

She wasn't sure it was true, though. Maybe Stephen had wanted to hurt and humiliate her for what she had done to him; she knew he was violently angry with her. Every time she saw him she was aware of the rage inside him, and she was an expert on hidden rage. She had lived with it for too many years not to recognise it in others.

But he hadn't hit her or hurt her physically, as Paolo suspected; any pain he had inflicted had been to her heart, not her body, and, anyway, she did not want Paolo to get into a fight with Stephen. The two men were not evenly matched; Stephen was bigger, fitter and more muscular—he could knock Paolo into the middle of next week without even trying.

'Satisfied?' Stephen snapped at Paolo.

'No, I'm damned well not! I heard a crash from in here; I heard her cry out when I was outside that door. It was a cry of pain—she'd been hurt and——'

He broke off as someone else knocked on the door, even louder and more peremptorily than the way in which he had knocked. They all started in surprise, turning to stare at the door.

'Now what?' grunted Stephen in a voice which sounded as if he was at the end of his tether. 'Who else are you expecting?'

'It's probably the room-service waiter, coming back for my breakfast tray,' she said shakily. Who else could it be?

Stephen strode across the room and flung the door open turning basilisk's eyes on whoever was outside. Gabriella was glad that she wasn't on the receiving end of that stare. 'What do you want?' he barked.

A furious, self-important voice answered him. 'I am the manager of this hotel, sir, and I have had a number of complaints about whatever has been happening in this room!'

Gabriella's heart sank.

'You'd better come in, then,' Stephen said curtly, stepping aside to let him pass.

The manager strutted into the room—a short, tubby, grey-haired man in a well-cut dark suit and silvery tie. He looked at Gabriella with disdain, running a look up and down her faintly dishevelled figure, and then gave the two men the same sort of glance, his nostrils pinched, his mouth set in an expression of distaste and offence.

'This is a respectable hotel; we do not expect our guests to have fights in their rooms, or shout and yell at each other. You have upset all the other guests on this floor.

'My reception clerk told me he had doubts about accepting the young lady as a guest when she first arrived because she did not seem to be the sort of client we wish to welcome to our hotel. However, she said she was touring, and was very tired, and would only want the room for one night—and he felt sorry for her. But it seems that he was quite right in his first impression.' He turned back to Gabriella, sniffing again. 'I shall have to ask you to leave my hotel at once.'

Gabriella was stricken with shame and embarrassment; she went white then red, wishing the floor would open up and swallow her. The feeling was bitterly familiar. This had happened to her before. Long ago, when she was still a child, she had been looked at with this terrible distaste and contempt, and she had wanted to die.

Stephen bit out fiercely, 'How dare you speak to her like that? You'll regret this! Get your things, Gabriella; I'm taking you back to England——'

Paolo broke in over his voice, 'No, she is not going back to England; she is coming to stay with me, at the Villa Caterina Bella, aren't you, Gabriella?'

The manager started violently, looking like someone who'd been hit round the face with a fish. He stared at Paolo, his black eyes round and incredulous. 'The Caterina Bella? You are not the owner of the Caterina Bella! What are you talking about?'

'I didn't say I was the owner. I said I was staying there—not that that is any business of yours!'

The round black eyes grew even rounder. 'You are a friend of...?'

'Yes,' said Paolo with curt unfriendliness. 'I work with the maestro—we are old friends. He has lent me his villa for a while, but he will be joining me shortly. I know he will be very shocked to hear how you have treated my cousin.'

'Cousin...?' repeated the manager unhappily, swallowing. 'The young lady is your cousin?'

'Yes.' Paolo turned to her. 'Pack your case, Gabriella; I will take you to the villa at once.'

Flushed and gabbling, the manager broke in, 'No, please. I see now that there has been a misunderstanding. A family quarrel...well, of course, that is different. I thought the young lady was entertaining men in her bedroom and...'

He gave her a sideways look, very red, shrugging apologetically. Gabriella then realised what he had thought she was; it was even worse than she had realised, even closer to meriting the disgust she had once seen in her grandmother's eyes, the hatred she had seen in her aunt's face. Burning colour rushed up to her hairline.

'Please forgive me!' The manager bowed to Gabriella. 'I am very sorry, *signorina*, if I have offended you. It is all the fault of my receptionist; he gave me the wrong impression...and the complaints of other guests... You know, a hotel like this has to be so careful—we cannot afford to get the wrong reputation. Please overlook what has happened. I hope you will stay on with us, and give us a chance to make up for this very stupid mistake.'

She made a helpless gesture. She was still upset and embarrassed, but she was too honest not to see his point of view. He was doing his job, protecting the reputation of the hotel. This was a discreet, civilised place. The air of tranquillity was soothing. That, after all, was what she had loved about it from the minute she had arrived, and she could understand why the hotel would not want that peace torn up by uproar and scenes, offending all those guests who had come here, like her, in search of a restful holiday.

She had seen the looks on the faces of the people in the corridor a little while ago. Most of the guests were middle-aged. This was that sort of hotel. It did not want children running up and down the corridors; it did not have a cabaret at night, or encourage loud music in the rooms. The atmosphere of the place was maintained by insisting on quietness and courtesy.

The manager took her gesture for agreement. 'Thank *you* for being so understanding, *signorina*.' He bowed. 'And if there is anything I can do, at any time, please do not hesitate to ask.' He turned to Paolo, his face eager. 'I am myself an opera fan, *signore*, I have many times been to productions by the maestro. Such a genius! It must be so fascinating to work with him.'

Gabriella felt a bubble of hysteria form in her throat and swallowed to keep it down. One minute he was ready to throw her out, the next he was desperately eager to keep her staying here, and it was not because he had realised that he had been mistaken about her, or because she and Paolo were cousins—it was Paolo's connections that had done the trick.

That was what fame did for you. You could get away with murder if you knew the right people!

'The Villa Caterina Bella is one of our most beautiful houses,' the manager was saying now. 'Are you staying there all summer?'

'Yes,' Paolo nodded. 'I'm having a working holiday. I design sets for the maestro and I'm painting frescos for him in his little theatre. Have you ever seen it?'

'Indeed I have, several times—the villa is open to visitors, as you know, one day a week, for charity. I remember the theatre—very beautiful, a little gem,' the manager said, beaming. 'So you are painting frescos on the walls—how exciting. May I ask what sort of frescos you are painting?'

'Scenes from famous operas and views of the lakes,' said Paolo, with a dry note in his voice which told Gabriella that he was well aware of the cause of the manager's change of attitude.

'How interesting. I shall look forward to seeing them when they are finished,' the manager said unctuously. 'And the maestro will be joining you later, you said? He usually does spend the summer here, of course.'

'Yes, he plans to be here before long, to go over plans for the next season with me and the musical director, who will be joining us too, at the villa.'

Paolo sounded polite and friendly, but when he met Gabriella's eyes she saw irony in his, and he winked at her discreetly. She looked away, her mouth quivering.

The plump little manager eagerly said, 'Perhaps, when he does arrive, one evening you would all be my guests here at the hotel for dinner? I have a marvellous chef—he would create a superb meal for the maestro. It would be a great honour.'

'I shall certainly mention it to the maestro,' Paolo said blandly, and for the first time Gabriella realised the sort of world Paolo now inhabited, the way his mind had changed, had developed, how far he had come from the shy, silent little boy she had grown up with in Brindisi. They had both come from hardworking, ordinary families. They had had few toys, no other friends and they had known very little of the world in those days.

Today, Paolo lived and breathed in a very different environment. He was not the same person she had once known. It had been stupid of her to imagine he could be. The serious-minded little boy had become a sophisticated, experienced man of the world used to moving in powerful circles, used to flattery and manipulation and privilege.

She felt a pang of loss; there was a gulf between them now. Their friendship belonged to another world, another time.

The hotel manager glanced at Stephen and his manner suddenly changed again as another thought occurred to him. No doubt he had picked up on the hostility between Paolo and Stephen. His black eyes like glinting little stones, he asked, 'Perhaps...

Was this man responsible for the incident? Has he been causing trouble? Would you like him to leave, *signorina*?'

Stephen's long, lean body was as tense as a bowstring, his grey eyes hard and dangerous.

'And are *you* going to make me leave?' he asked him, his lips scarcely moving, the words bitten out between his teeth.

The manager was not a brave man; he backed, going pale. 'I . . . I shall call the porter . . .'

Gabriella had to intervene before another scene started. She hurriedly said, 'No! This gentleman is my fiancé, *signore*!'

Stephen quickly glanced down at her, his eyes narrowing at the claim. She had told him that she would not marry him. She had run away from him, yet here she was claiming him as her fiancé! A fiery spark lit his dark pupils.

She met his gaze imploringly, desperate not to have any more trouble. For a second his mouth parted, as if he was going to make some sarcastic or revealing comment, then his shoulders moved in a shrug.

'That's right; we are about to get married,' he said in a calmer tone.

The manager was taken aback. 'Married?' he repeated, dark red.

Paolo intervened again. 'Ah, *signore*—we are all Italians; we know what family life is like! The quarrels, the making up, the fights, the kissing . . . pure opera! Family life and opera are never far apart in Italy.'

The manager gave a nervous little laugh, covered in confusion now. 'You are right, *signore*. Yes, indeed, the opera and the family are both very important to us.' He gestured with his hands, gabbling apologetically at Stephen. 'Ah, *la famiglia ... Scusi, scusi, mi dispiace, signore ...*'

Stephen inclined his head without a word, his strong features grim.

'And now we must be on our way; we're lunching at the villa,' said Paolo, even more amused. He looked at his watch. 'It's gone twelve! Come along, Gabriella; my car's parked outside.'

She gave him a grateful smile—tactful, clever Paolo; he thought fast on his feet. 'I'd like to change first, though,' she said, gesturing at her rumpled clothes.

'Of course.' Paolo opened the door and gestured to the other two men. 'We'll wait for you downstairs in the lounge, Gabriella. Don't take too long, though, will you?'

The manager muttered something polite in Italian and gratefully rushed away, glad to escape from the embarrassment of his situation. Stephen gave her one long, insistent stare, then he went too, and Paolo followed him out, giving her a little grin before he closed the door.

Left alone, Gabriella sank down on the side of the bed, closing her eyes with a little moan of exhaustion. She felt as if she had been through a wringer. The last thing she wanted to do was have lunch with Paolo at the Villa Caterina Bella, but she didn't want to stay here at the hotel either.

Well, she couldn't sit here all day, much as she would have liked to. She had to change her clothes, make herself more presentable—she must look as if she had been dragged through a hedge backwards.

She stripped off her top and jeans and went into the bathroom in her bra and panties to wash again; she felt grubby, her body damp with perspiration after all that had happened since she got up. Was that only such a short time ago? It seemed like days since she had first opened her eyes to a radiantly lovely morning. She had felt so peaceful then, but that wonderful feeling of calm happiness had not lasted long, had it? Just long enough for Stephen to get here! Peace had flown out of the window once he had arrived.

She had a quick shower, which certainly improved her state of mind, then went back into her bedroom and changed into something less casual—a spring-green dress with a scalloped neckline, a close-fitting bodice, tight waist tied with a wide sash at the back, and a calf-length, full, flowing skirt. She didn't hurry doing her make-up and hair—if the manager was downstairs, or she ran into some of the other guests, she wanted to be certain that she looked her best.

It was a quarter of an hour later when she walked out of the lift downstairs. She found Paolo and Stephen standing by the window looking out over the terraced gardens towards the lake. They had their backs to her and were absorbed in conversation; for a minute she was relieved to see that they did not seem about to come to blows but then she wondered with a prickle of anxiety what they were talking about. Her?

As she walked towards them they heard her footsteps on the marble floor and swung to face her, standing side by side.

She felt the world shift, her whole being disorientated, dislocated as she looked into their faces—the only two men in the world who had ever been close to her. Then the fractured pieces came together again and the world stopped swinging wildly; she saw clearly again, saw the two men she loved—one as a brother, the other as a lover—and her heart turned over in joy and pain.

Loving was both. She was still afraid of feeling like this, afraid of the way it might end. You gave a hostage to fortune when you loved someone, especially if you didn't understand them. You could get badly hurt. She had been once, and it had not been her fault, yet she had been blamed for everything that had happened. How could she help being angry about that? She needed love so badly, yet she was afraid to reach for it because of the past—no wonder rage churned inside her every time she thought about it.

'You look lovely,' Paolo said gently, smiling at her, and she felt the angry tension draining out of her; her mouth trembled into an answering smile. The familiar Paolo she had known all her life was back—the friend she trusted, not the strange, discomfiting stranger who moved in a world of sophistication and cynicism. Perhaps there were two Paolos? Perhaps beneath the shell of the man who had changed so much there still hid the shy little boy who had had no other friend but her?

'Thank you, Paolo,' she said with affection and relief. She would have missed him if the Paolo she had known had really gone forever; he was the last link with a life which had otherwise vanished, the world of her childhood, when she had been happy with both her parents, safe and loved and filled with all the blind optimism of innocence.

Stephen didn't say anything, but his eyes made her pulses beat with fire as they moved over her, from her smoothly brushed head, her bright, spring-like dress to the rise of her high breasts, the curve of her waist and hips, her long, slender legs.

She took a quick, shaky breath. Every time they were in the same room he had that effect on her; she responded to him the same way she did to light, air, music—instinctively, immediately, with passion—and even fear couldn't change that. She almost wished it could, because she was so tired of getting hurt.

'You're both driving back to the villa with me; Stephen will leave his car here at the hotel,' Paolo told her, holding out his hand. 'Come on, Gabriella—I've arranged a really special lunch; you'll enjoy this.' There was mischief in his eyes and she laughed.

'What have you been up to now?'

'Wait and see!' He seized her hand and pulled her along with him, past the reception desk where the clerk stared at Paolo, getting up to bow to him.

'*Buongiorno, signore*!'

Paolo answered him with a faint smile, a touch
of wry cynicism in his eyes. How did it feel to get
that sort of reception once people knew you worked
for someone famous? wondered Gabriella. Did it
irritate Paolo? Or was he accustomed to it, re-
signed to it?

His car was parked right outside; he opened the
rear door and held it open for Gabriella. She slid
inside, and Stephen got in from the other door.
Paolo closed the door again, and Gabriella flicked
a sideways look at Stephen's impassive face. 'What
were you and Paolo talking about while I was
getting ready?'

'You,' he said coolly. 'What else?'

What else indeed? she thought, her nerves beating
with tension. She'd known they had to be talking
about her, but she still did not like it.

'What about me?'

Paolo had stopped to speak to the hotel porter,
pointing to Stephen's car. They could hear him explaining that it would be left there for some time—
Stephen was not a guest but he was visiting a guest
in the hotel. The porter began to argue. Paolo fished
a banknote out of his pocket and handed it to the
porter who smilingly nodded, pocketing it.

Stephen said quietly, 'I took the opportunity of
asking Paolo about your childhood and your Italian
family—he's the only person who could tell me
about all that. You never have, have you?'

The dryness of his tone made her look away. 'I
told you about my parents.'

The defensive note in her voice made his mouth
twist with cynicism. 'You mentioned them, but you

never told me anything about yourself; I had to prise every syllable out of you. And even now there's still so much I don't know, isn't there, Gabriella?'

Inside her the dark rage flared again. 'What have you ever told me?' she threw back. 'What do I know about you?'

Paolo opened the driver's door and got behind the wheel at that instant and Stephen didn't answer her.

'I've asked the porter to keep an eye on your car,' Paolo told him in Italian and Stephen thanked him in the same language, smoothly polite suddenly, and very formal.

'*Tante grazie. Le sono molto obligato.*'

What had changed? What had they said to each other while she was upstairs changing? She felt a childish resentment; she did not want them to be friends, especially when they excluded her.

Leaning back in the corner of the car, she turned her whole body away, staring out as they drove along the narrow, meandering road through the village towards the Villa Caterina Bella. Between the white-walled, rose-pink-roofed houses on her left she saw the blue gleam of the lake and above that the brilliant blue sky, cloudless at the moment.

Rising behind it were the white-capped peaks of the mountains on the other side of the lake. As usual, there was a ferry crossing from one side to the other, from Bellagio to Menaggio.

It was so beautiful here; she wished she were in the same calm, reflective mood as the landscape she was staring at, but she wasn't. She was in the same turmoil of uncertainty and anger that she had been in for days now.

Paolo suddenly slowed and turned off the road, in front of closed, wrought-iron gates. There was a little man with a bald head and a wrinkled, weathered face clipping hedges beyond them; he looked round at the car, then came trotting forward, producing a bunch of great keys from the pocket of his navy blue gardening-apron. He unlocked the gates, pulled them open, and stood back, smiling cheerfully as Paolo drove in past him.

Slowing, Paolo thanked him. '*Tante grazie*, Giovanni.'

'*Prego*, Signor Giovio,' the old man said, closing the gates.

Gabriella sat up and leaned forward to look out, staring up through dark green cypress and yew trees to the golden stone of the romantic nineteenth-century façade of the house. Set among smooth lawns and great banks of pink and yellow rhodo-dendrons, azaleas and huge, shiny-leaved camellia bushes glowing with red and white blossoms, the villa was unreal—so lovely that it floated like a dream among its gaudy flowers, shimmering and incandescent.

They drove a little further on, then Paolo parked and turned to look at her and Stephen.

'Why don't you two wander around, explore the gardens, while I check on lunch? Walk up to the house in about half an hour and we'll be ready for you.'

'We can do that later,' Gabriella began, her nerves prickling at the idea of being alone with

Stephen again, but the latter had already got out, slamming the door behind him, and was rapidly coming round to her side of the car. She looked in agitation at Paolo. 'I don't want to stay out here with him!'

'Don't be such a coward!' Paolo told her drily. 'If you don't want to marry him, say so—but don't just try to avoid the subject. Stop hiding from life, Gabriella; face up to it.'

She flushed angrily. 'I'm not hiding from anything!'

Stephen opened the car door. 'Come on, out you get!'

She glared at him. 'Will you stop ordering me around?' But she couldn't go on arguing—it would be too humiliating. She might as well get it over with, tell Stephen firmly that she wasn't going to marry him and send him away. Giving Paolo a reproachful look, she turned and slid out. Stephen closed the door firmly and the car moved on up the drive at a steady five or so miles an hour, the wheels crunching on the gravel.

Beside the drive a path wound away between blossoming dogwood, slender trees whose branches were frothy with pink and white. Slowly she began to walk along the mossy, sandy path below the branches, and Stephen fell into step beside her.

'Paolo tells me these gardens are world-famous,' he murmured coolly. 'The colours are breathtaking, aren't they? I suppose the soil here must be very acid or these azaleas and rhododendrons wouldn't do so well. Don't they come from the Himalayas originally?'

'Is that what you want to talk to me about? Gardens?' She stood still to stare down through the trees and shrubs at the blue of the lake, glittering like a jewel in the sunlight. From up here they couldn't hear the traffic on the busy road beneath; they were wrapped in peace and beauty, yet Gabriella still felt that terrible anger burning inside her.

'Why don't you go away and leave me alone?' she burst out hoarsely, turning on him. 'I hate the sight of you, can't you understand that? I ran away because I never wanted to see you again. I just want you out of my life.'

Stephen looked as if he had turned to stone. He stared at her fixedly, his face colourless, unmoving, blank, like the face of a statue, eyeless and dead.

After what seemed an eternity he turned and began to walk away.

He was going. He was leaving her.

Agony pierced her. Tears stung her eyes. He was walking out of her life forever, and she wished she were dead.

CHAPTER NINE

THEN Stephen stopped dead in his tracks and stood there with his back to her, his black head bent as if he was staring at something on the ground. She watched him, trembling. What now? His head came up and he swung round and began to walk back towards her with long, angry strides, his whole body pulsating with a rage she could feel even from a hundred paces away.

Gabriella tensed with a peculiar mixture of alarm, hope and confusion. She was afraid of the pain loving him could bring, yet she couldn't bear to see him go, and, torn between one and the other anguish, she was in a state of utter chaos. She would have fled if there had been time, but he reached her before she could decide what to do.

The only defence she had was words. 'Don't you touch me!' she hurriedly said, and saw his eyes flash.

'Touch you?' he repeated in a horse, ragged voice. 'I haven't even started on you yet.'

This close she could see his face clearly; it looked strange, unfamiliar, the strong features convulsed with an emotion she couldn't identify for certain—was it pain or rage or desire? Whichever it was, the feelings were powerful and disturbing.

Gabriella backed and Stephen advanced inexorably, staring at her with fixed intensity.

'You aren't sending me away like that! Hate me or not, I'm not going until I know for sure...'

'What?' she whispered as he stopped, still staring at her. 'Until you know what?'

She couldn't back any further; she felt a hedge behind her now, the leaves rustling and brushing against her.

'An answer to one question.'

'What question?'

Stephen's hands came up and reached for her, grabbed her upper arms and pulled her forward so abruptly that she lost her balance and fell towards him.

'This,' he muttered, and her pulses went crazy as she saw his head coming down.

'No...' she groaned, looking at the strong, male lines of his mouth as it descended.

'Yes,' he said huskily, and kissed her angrily, fiercely, his mouth hurting her.

She fought him, pulling her head back from the onslaught of his mouth, punching him in the chest with both hands curled into fists. He ignored her for a moment or two, his hard mouth insistent, until she began to kick his ankles.

Her toe must have connected because Stephen gave a little grunt of pain, and finally broke off the kiss, but held on to her, looking down at her furious face. Tears glittered in her eyes, her skin was dark red and she was shaking with resentment as she lifted a hand to her mouth, felt the bruised heat where his mouth had crushed it.

'You bastard! That hurt, and you did it deliberately; you knew what you were doing! You wanted to hurt me!'

'What do you think you've done to me?' he threw back, the lines of his face clenched with pain and rage. 'First you walk out on me on our wedding-day without an explanation, making me a laughing-stock in front of my friends, and now, just when I thought I was making progress, finding out what was wrong all this time, getting to know you properly at last, you turn on me as if I were your enemy, tell me to get out of your life for good, and tell me you hate me! How did you expect me to take that? Aren't I allowed to have any feelings? What do you take me for? Some sort of machine?'

She was trembling, frightened by his anger yet at the same time still possessed by her own secret rage, the mind-clouding emotion she was only now admitting that she had felt ever since she was a young girl. All those years ago she had felt guilty about what had happened with her uncle, and at the same time she had always known that she was not to blame. No wonder that, mind and body, she was a battleground of contrary, bewildering emotions that she could never resolve. No wonder rage had driven her ever since she had met Stephen and found herself trapped in another emotional conflict.

Her voice low and unsteady, she whispered, 'I don't think I know you at all.'

'No,' he bit out. 'I don't think you do either, but you're going to, Gabriella; believe me, you're going

to. I don't give up easily, especially when I want
something as badly as I want you.'

She bitterly threw back at him, 'Want? Want? Is
that all you understand? I'm not some company
you're trying to acquire! I'm a woman, a human
being...'

'Oh, I know you're a woman,' he muttered, his
eyes half closing, his voice huskily aroused as he
looked down at her, and she felt her body quiver
with passion at the expression on his face.

'S-stop it,' she stammered, trying to pull away.

'Stop what?'

'Looking at me.'

'Can't I even look at you now?' he angrily
mocked, his mouth twisted and bitter.

'Not like that!'

'Like what, Gabriella?' he asked in that deep,
husky voice, and his eyes were molten with desire.
She stared into them, shuddering, with heat inside
her. Her mind swam with confusion—she was terrified by the hunger she saw in those eyes, and yet
she felt an echo of his desire deep inside her.

'As if you...'

'As if I what? Want to do this?'

He slowly bent his head and she stiffened, but
this time his mouth did not hurt; he was not angry
now. His mouth didn't even touch her at first; instead she felt his tongue-tip softly caress her bruised
and aching lips, move very slowly, very softly, along
the trembling curve of her mouth, over and over
again, soothing, comforting, but above all so
sensual that she groaned, her mouth parting with
the deep sigh of her pleasure.

His tongue slid inside. She groaned again, her body instinctively moving closer to his, swaying into him, her mouth clinging to his, and then his arms went round her and held her even closer as the kiss deepened and took fire.

When he broke off the kiss again she didn't try to move away; she leaned on him, trembling with the passion he had unleashed. Stephen watched her through those half-closed lids; there was a dark red heat in his face and his eyes were brilliant with feeling.

'I love you, Gabriella,' he said softly, and her breathing seemed to stop.

She stared at him, her eyes stretched wide, unknowingly shaking her head; afraid to believe him.

'Yes,' he said, looking at her with the same intense passion that she had seen in his eyes before. 'I've been in love with you almost since the day I first saw you. I took one look and thought I'd found the woman I'd been waiting for all my life. You were everything I wanted in a woman, Gabriella, and you weren't just beautiful; your eyes held such intelligence, and you had a shy, gentle smile.'

Her heart beat so fast that she felt dizzy. 'You never said anything like this before,' she whispered. 'If it's true, why didn't you tell me?'

His mouth twisted. 'I'm not blind, or stupid. I knew you weren't in love with me, that the lightning hadn't struck you the way it had struck me on first sight.

'I thought at first that I'd just have to wait for you to fall in love, but then I began to realise there were problems hidden under your lovely face. I began to see that you were scared stiff of intimacy for some reason. You wouldn't confide in me, and I didn't know the right questions to ask, did I? So I couldn't find out what made you so screwed up inside, so frightened of showing your feelings, but I knew you weren't indifferent. When I kissed you, I knew I was getting a response.'

She blushed, her lashes hiding her eyes, and he laughed softly.

'Yes. I thought at first that you were just plain scared of sex, but there was something else, I began to realise. I didn't dare risk trying to get you into bed, because I didn't know what sort of hornets' nest I might arouse, but your responses whenever I did touch you made me hopeful—and you went on seeing me.

'I told myself that if you didn't like me you wouldn't date me. We seemed to get on well—we could talk, we liked the same things... I thought, give it time; be patient.'

Gabriella gave him a sudden wry smile. 'Patient? You?' It was not a virtue he was famous for. Energy, drive, determination—all these he possessed in abundance—but patience? No, never.

He grimaced, half laughing. 'I think I was very patient with you, Gabriella. I was amazed by myself, in fact. I tried to get you to talk about whatever was wrong several times, but you always got so tense that I gave up trying. But I fell deeper and deeper in love with you, and I'm a normal male—I was desperate to make love to you; it was driving me crazy not getting you into bed.'

She trembled at the passion in his voice, and he bent his head to put his lips against her throat, whispering close to her ear.

'God, Gabriella, if you knew how much I love you, how much I need you...'

She shut her eyes, hearing his deep, thickened voice echoing inside her head.

'I thought... if there was no hope for a future with you then I had to know that. It was killing me not to know where I stood with you. So I risked asking you to marry me,' he muttered. 'I knew it was a gamble. I was terrified you'd refuse and then stop seeing me, but I had to know what my chances were. And you accepted. That was when I realised that it wasn't sex you were so scared of—you'd never have promised to marry me if it had been. You must have known I'd expect you to go to bed with me.'

He put a finger beneath her chin and pushed her head up; she opened her eyes and looked back at him, very flushed.

'I'm right, aren't I?' he asked softly.

She nodded, her mouth too dry for her to be able to speak.

'You weren't scared of sex itself?'

'No.' She sighed. 'I wish it had just been sex... that would have been simpler to deal with! If I'd been raped by a stranger, for instance, I'm sure I could eventually have talked about it; I could have gone to see a therapist, and had treatment; I'd have realised it wasn't my fault. I wouldn't have been so ashamed of that—I could have talked it out, but the truth was so much worse...'

He said fiercely, 'Gabriella, what happened wasn't your fault!'

She looked at him with anguish, her voice breaking. 'I tell myself that all the time, but deep down I don't believe it; deep down I feel guilty. I blame myself.'

His face tightened, dark with anger. 'Because of your damned family!'

'Yes,' she said, white to her hairline. 'They never forgave me—my grandmother, my aunt...'

'They were the ones who should be ashamed! You were just a child; you were the victim; you were guilty of nothing but a child's need to be loved.'

'But I was no longer a child; they were right. I was almost a grown-up.'

'Stop telling yourself that! It isn't true! It never was. At thirteen you were still half a child, but he was a grown man; he knew he had no right to feel that way about you. He should have protected you, not tried to seduce you.'

A sob caught in her throat and Stephen held her closer, his head against her hair.

'Don't cry, darling. Don't.' He kissed her hair, put his cheek against it. 'It breaks my heart to see that look in your eyes, to hear you cry. I love you so much, Gabriella.'

She drew a shaky breath, leaning on him, clinging to him. She felt a strange, new comfort in having his arms around her, in feeling his love surrounding her, hearing the deep feeling in his voice.

'When we get back to England I'm going to arrange for you to go into analysis,' he said quietly.

'You need to talk this out; you need to face it all and get rid of the guilt, Gabriella. You can't live with it for the rest of your life. You've buried it— that was your mistake. It never works to bury feelings of that sort—they just fester and poison the whole of your life. As soon as we get back from our honeymoon you'll start having sessions with a therapist.'

She stiffened and pushed him away, looking at him wildly. 'What do you mean, "honeymoon"? I told you... I can't marry you.'

'Don't you love me, Gabriella?' he asked softly, and she froze, her eyes wide, naked with feeling.

Stephen smiled at her.

'Don't!' she cried out, trembling.

'Tell me you don't love me, Gabriella!'

She covered her face with her hands. 'I can't...'

'Can't tell me? You aren't still afraid of me, are you? You can tell me anything, Gabriella.'

'I can't love you!' she groaned, and he took her hands and pulled them down.

'Look at me when you say that, darling.'

He tipped back her head and made her look at him, and Gabriella, eyes wet and wide, stared at him with her heart in her eyes. She heard his intake of breath and then he put his arms around her and held her close against him, his head on her hair.

'I'll make you happy; I swear I'll make you happy,' he whispered, and then he pushed her hair back from her face and kissed her forehead, her eyes, her cheek, her mouth, murmuring to her all the time. 'I love you, Gabriella. I can be patient if I have to; I'll wait to marry you if you really aren't ready to go through with it yet, but just don't make me wait too long because I love you so much it's killing me.'

She began to kiss him back with passion, winding her arms around his neck, and he groaned out her name.

Suddenly he pulled back, looking down at her with wry, passionate eyes. 'We'd better go up to the house for lunch now, before I lose my head again.'

Very flushed, laughing, she let him take her hand, and they walked up through the magnificent gardens towards the Villa Caterina Bella.

Paolo met them on the top terrace, which was paved with marble and surrounded by a white stone balustrade. He was leaning elegantly at the top of the short flight of steps which led up to the terrace, and waved to them as they emerged from behind a little cluster of magnolia trees, the waxy white blossoms like chalices uplifted to the sun.

'I wondered if I should send out a search party,' he murmured, grinning at them.

'Sorry, are we late?' Stephen returned blandly, and Paolo gave him a dry look.

'A little, but never mind. Did you admire the gardens?'

Stephen looked blank. 'The gardens? Oh, yes, the gardens ... they're ravishing.'

'I've never seen anything so beautiful in my life,' Gabriella chimed in hurriedly, and Paolo smiled at her with affectionate amusement.

'I thought you'd like them. Come and have lunch.'

To their surprise, instead of leading them into the villa he began to walk around the house. As they fell in beside him, Gabriella asked, 'Where are we going?'

'I thought you'd like a picnic today, so I've had a cold buffet laid out in one of the conservatories. We'll sit on a lawn near by and eat the food in the open air.'

'That sounds marvellous.' She paused as they rounded the house and saw the smooth green lawns and flowerbeds behind it. 'Oh, how pretty!'

'Isn't it. Very English, this part of the gardens. The conservatory is Victorian, by the way, designed by a Scotsman, rather in the style of the Crystal Palace, I gather.'

It was an amazing building—the glass arches of the roof glittered in the sunlight, and, inside, a small fountain of water sparkled as it rose and fell among the semi-tropical plants which the conservatory housed.

Paolo opened the door and they followed him inside to find that a long trestle-table had been covered with a white cloth on which was laid out a series of plates and dishes filled with food—cold chicken, a platter of various cold meats, sliced Italian salami and sausages, a game pie which had been cut into quarters, bowls of different salads including pasta and rice, boiled eggs, cheese and fruit.

'There's enough here to feed ten of us!' protested Gabriella, putting salad on to her plate. Paolo used tongs to lay slices of meat on her plate too.

'It won't be wasted. What's left will go back into the fridge to be used for my supper.' He was about to pick up some rice to put on her plate but she stopped him.

'I've got more than enough, thank you, Paolo!'

They ate their food on the smooth, billiard-table-like lawn outside, where Paolo had spread a Stuart tartan rug and dark green velvet cushions for them to sit on. They drank champagne and orange juice, had grapes and peaches to follow the salad, and afterwards Paolo produced cups and saucers and a vacuum flask of coffee.

The sun was so warm that Gabriella lay down with her head on a cushion and could almost have fallen asleep, listening to the quiet murmur of the men's voices, the splash of the fountain in the conservatory, the hum of bees among the flowers.

Suddenly she heard Paolo say, 'Why don't you get married here?' and she shot up, eyes wide and startled.

'What?'

'That's a very good idea,' Stephen said slowly. 'But it might be difficult—there are bound to be problems, marrying in a foreign country.'

'Gabriella is half Italian; she has an Italian passport. This isn't a foreign country to her—she was born and brought up here,' Paolo pointed out.

'We can't,' she protested, and Stephen turned to look at her, his eyes tender.

'It would solve one major problem.'

'What are you talking about?'

'The embarrassment of announcing our marriage *again*!'

'Oh,' she said, biting her lip.

'And knowing that people will be wondering if you're going to run off again,' he added drily.

She blushed. 'I hadn't thought of that.'

'I had,' he said, his mouth twisting. 'I would have a very uneasy feeling until I finally managed to put that ring on your finger!'

She looked helplessly at him. 'I'm so sorry, Stephen. It must have been awful for you.'

'She may be half Italian,' he said to Paolo, 'but she has managed to inherit the English genius for understatement.'

Paolo laughed. 'Ah, but the Italian side of her is far more exciting, Stephen. Don't worry. Look, why not get married here, in Como? I can fix it all up for you. The maestro's name opens all doors here—he's a living legend; he can do anything he wants to! I'll talk to him and we'll create the most beautiful wedding that ever happened in this world, and you and Gabriella don't have to do anything about it.'

'My wedding-dress is back in London!' she protested.

'It can be brought here by your cousin Lara,' Paolo quickly said. 'She'll be delighted to come, won't she?'

She couldn't deny that; Lara would jump at the chance to have a trip to the Italian lakes.

'How soon could it happen?' asked Stephen, and Paolo shrugged.

'I don't know, but it shouldn't take long.'

Stephen looked at her, his eyes dark and pleading. 'Gabriella?'

He was leaving the decision to her, and she hesitated, her mind in confusion. She wanted to be his wife, she wanted to be with him, but what if that panic swept over her again? She stared at Stephen, saw the little tic beating beside his mouth, the pallor of his skin, and love swamped everything else. She smiled at him with passion, and nodded.

Stephen let out a long, relieved, triumphant breath.

They were married three weeks later, on the lawns behind the Villa Caterina Bella, with all the arrangements orchestrated by Paolo. It was a much quieter wedding than the one which had originally been planned in London—only family and close friends flew out from England to be there, and there was a sprinkling of Gabriella's Italian relatives, who managed the drive from Brindisi to be present.

Lara was there, of course, and was the matron of honour as planned, and the bridesmaids managed to get time off from work for the wedding too.

'You certainly made this a memorable wedding!' they teased Gabriella as they helped her get ready on the morning itself. 'Running off like that, and then changing your mind again! Nobody is going to forget your wedding, that's for sure.'

'Sorry,' she said, her mind more on getting her veil to hang the right way than on what they were saying.

'I even had reporters badgering me on the phone,' ice-blonde Jilly said. 'My old dad was utterly shocked.'

Knowing that Jilly's father trained racehorses and was a friend of royalty, Gabriella could imagine his reaction to seeing his daughter's name in gossip columns, even if by association.

'She's only teasing you,' Petra comforted, her spiky black hair smoothed down for once and

bearing a crown of fresh white rosebuds. She made
a face at Jilly. 'Stop it, Jilly; she always takes you
seriously, you know that! Don't upset her on her
wedding-day—it's bad luck!'

Jilly gave Gabriella a quick look. 'Sorry, darling;
I was only joking, you know! Dad sent his love and
hoped you'd be very happy.'

Petra moved to the window to look out. 'Your
cousin Paolo is very efficient; he's out there at the
marquee, organising everything like mad. Darling,
he's fabulous—is there a woman in his life?'

'Not that he's ever told me about.'

'He isn't gay, is he?'

Gabriella laughed. 'Why don't you ask him?'

'I will,' Petra decided, still lingering to watch
Paolo. 'These theatrical types often are, but he's
Italian.'

'What's that got to do with it?' Jilly impatiently
demanded.

'You know ... Italians ... they're supposed to be
very hot-blooded, aren't they?'

Gabriella and Jilly laughed. 'I'll tell Paolo your
theory,' Gabriella said, adjusting the set of her
head-dress. 'How does that look?'

'Better,' Jilly nodded.

'I bet Stephen is,' said Petra.

Confused, Gabriella stared at her. 'Is what?'

'Hot-blooded.'

Gabriella blushed, and at that second Lara arrived with an opened bottle of champagne and a
tray of glasses.

'Here you are—I thought you'd feel better for a
little buzz, and there's nothing like champagne for
giving you that.' She poured four glasses; they all

took one and Lara lifted hers in a toast. 'Enjoy your day, Gabriella, and be happy ever after.'

Gabriella smiled at them as they all sipped champagne. 'Thanks, and thanks for forgiving me for ruining your day last time, and for coming all this way now.'

'It's wonderful,' said Petra, sighing as she looked out of the window again into the gardens of the villa. 'What a romantic setting for a wedding. I walked by the lake early this morning and I couldn't believe how beautiful it was . . . seeing the sun come up behind the mountains, the red glow reflected in the lake. It's heaven here, darling, and it's heaven staying here in this gorgeous villa. Thanks for asking us to come.'

Gabriella drained her glass of the golden sparkling wine and felt the brilliance of it entering her veins. The weather was superb, the views from the villa magical—Petra was right; this was a far more romantic setting than she would have had in London.

Then Lara said, 'I'll take Jilly and Petra downstairs now, then, darling, to give you a few minutes alone before you have to come down too.'

They all kissed her and wished her luck and told her how radiant she looked, how beautiful in her wedding-dress.

Then they had gone, chattering and giggling, and she was alone, the door shut and silence descending. She was afraid to sit down in case she crushed her dress; she looked down at the full crinoline skirt with its scattered pale pink satin rosebuds, and moved to set it swaying and dipping. It felt wonderful as she walked, but sitting down in

it was not easy. She looked at herself in the mirror
to make a final check and barely recognised herself.
That was not her, it was "the bride". With her
wedding-dress she had put on a symbolic persona
which hid the real person inside it. She hadn't expected that.

While she was thinking about this, Paolo
knocked on the door and asked, 'Are you ready,
Gabriella?' and she suddenly had a sharp stab of
uncertainly, of doubt, of fear.

She wasn't ready. She wasn't sure that she would
ever be ready. She froze on the spot, as white as
her dress.

'Gabriella?' Paolo knocked again, his voice
sounding anxious—no doubt he was wondering if
she was about to bolt again.

She swallowed down her nerves, huskily said,
'Yes, I'm coming,' and Paolo opened the door and
stood there staring at her.

To her dismay tears came into his eyes.

'Paolo, what is it?' she gasped.

'You look so lovely.' He took her hand and lifted
it to his lips. '*Cara*, be happy.'

She wanted to cry too. A bubble of tears seemed
about to burst in her throat. 'Oh, Paolo...' she
whispered.

He ceremonially placed her hand on his arm and
smiled at her, his mouth quivering.

'He's waiting for you, looking like a man about
to be shot—if you don't arrive in one minute he's
going to think you've run out on him again, so let's
start now, *cara*.'

He led her down the stairs and out into the
morning sunlight, into the marquee, filled with the

scent of a thousand flowers, with the sound of music and the light of candles, and Stephen turned his head sharply to look back down the aisle between the chairs, his face white with the fear that she was not coming.

Gabriella had her veil down over her face, so he could not see her, but the music swelled into a triumphal anthem, and Stephen took a long, deep breath of relief as she walked down the aisle towards him.

As he later put back her veil to see her face and kiss her on the mouth she saw the brilliance of his eyes, the passion and love which had frightened her so much, and suddenly she knew the fear had gone, and with it the anger she had felt for so long, the rage against what had happened to her all those years ago. She was free of the past. As Stephen bent to kiss her she met his mouth with passion.

'I love you,' he whispered huskily, and at last she could say it too, with all the emotion she had tried to hide for so long.

'I love you too, darling.'

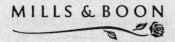

MILLS & BOON

PENNINGTON

Everyone's favourite town—delightful people,
prosperity and picturesque charm.

We know you'll love reading about this
charming English town in Catherine George's
latest Pennington novel:

Earthbound Angel

After her husband's death Imogen was lonely
in her cottage in the country. When Gabriel
came to do her gardening he seemed to
provide the answer. But could she risk an
affair? After all, Gabriel was her employee
and, surely younger than herself...

Available: March 1996

Happy
Mother's
Day

Don't miss this year's exciting Mother's Day Gift Pack—4 new heartwarming romances featuring three babies and a wedding!

The Right Kind of Girl	Betty Neels
The Baby Caper	Emma Goldrick
Part-Time Father	Sharon Kendrick
The Male Animal	Suzanne Carey

**This special Gift Pack of four romances
is priced at just £5.99**
(normal retail price £7.96)

 Available: February 1996   *Price:* £5.99

MILLS & BOON

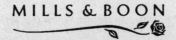

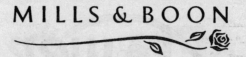

MILLS & BOON

Next Month's Romances

Each month you can choose from a wide variety of romance with Mills & Boon. Below are the new titles to look out for next month.

CLIMAX OF PASSION	Emma Darcy
MARRYING MARY	Betty Neels
EARTHBOUND ANGEL	Catherine George
A WEEKEND TO REMEMBER	Miranda Lee
HOLLYWOOD WEDDING	Sandra Marton
COMING HOME	Patricia Wilson
A CAREFUL WIFE	Lindsay Armstrong
FAST AND LOOSE	Elizabeth Oldfield
CHARLOTTE'S COWBOY	Jeanne Allan
SISTER OF THE BRIDE	Valerie Parv
ONE-NIGHT WIFE	Day Leclaire
HEARTLESS STRANGER	Elizabeth Duke
DANGEROUS GROUND	Alison Kelly
TENDER CAPTIVE	Rosemary Carter
BRIDE OF MY HEART	Rebecca Winters
TOO LATE FOR REGRETS	Liza Hadley

Fl🌸wer P🌸wer

How would you like to win a year's supply of simply irresistible romances? Well, you can and they're free! Simply unscramble the words below and send the completed puzzle to us by 31st August 1996. The first 5 correct entries picked after the closing date will win a years supply of Temptation novels (four books every month—worth over £100).

1	LTIUP	TULIP
2	FIDLADFO	
3	ERSO	
4	AHTNYHCI	
5	GIBANOE	
6	NEAPUTI	
7	YDSIA	
8	SIIR	
9	NNAIATCRO	
10	LDIAAH	
11	RRSEOIMP	
12	LEGXFOOV	
13	OYPPP	
14	LZEAAA	
15	COIRDH	

Please turn over for details of how to enter 🖝

Hw t enter

Listed overleaf are 15 jumbled-up names of flowers. All you
have to do is unscramble the names and write your answer in
the space provided. We've done the first one for you!

When you have found all the words, don't forget to fill in your
name and address in the space provided below and pop this
page into an envelope (you don't need a stamp) and post it
today. Hurry—competition ends 31st August 1996.

Mills & Boon Flower Puzzle
FREEPOST
Croydon
Surrey
CR9 3WZ

Are you a Reader Service Subscriber?   Yes ❑   No ❑

Ms/Mrs/Miss/Mr _____

Address _____

_____

_____ Postcode _____

One application per household.

You may be mailed with other offers from other reputable companies as
a result of this application. If you would prefer not to receive such offers,
please tick box. ❑

COMP396
B